PERFECT GIFTS

Harrisburg Railers, 12

RJ SCOTT
V.L. LOCEY

Love Lane Books

Copyright

All Rights Reserved

Perfect Gifts (Railers, 12)

Family comes first in all things. Whatever the cost.

Ten had always heard the saying, "Out of the mouths of babes," but he hadn't expected it to hit home as it had. After a comment from their daughter, Ten and Jared ponder an addition to the family. Moving into the adoption process is nerve-wracking and riddled with anxiety—kind of the way the Railers have been playing as of late. Bringing two young men into their homes and hearts won't be a smooth ride. But with patience, humor, and love, the bumpy road might just be a little easier to travel.

Expanding their small family was always in the cards, but no one could have foreseen the process clashing with the worst ever start to a Railers season. A string of losses, a vital player missing from the defense, a captain in the emergency room—and winning a single game seems impossible, let alone getting the team to the playoffs. Faced with hard decisions, Jared refuses to take his work home, but it's difficult when your husband is at the leading edge of the losing streak. His focus fractures when one sibling they're matched with is frustrated, angry, and has a healthy dose of mistrust. Jared and Ten's parenting skills are tested, but they'll do anything to make a place in their home the perfect gift for two children lost in the system.

Dedication

To my family who accepts me and all my foibles and quirks. Even the plastic banana in my holster.
VL Locey

Always for my family.
RJ Scott

Christmas
A RAILERS NOVELLA

PERFECT
Gifts

RJ SCOTT &
V.L. LOCEY

Love Lane Books

Chapter One

Ten

"Okay, so today we're going to listen to something new," I said, taking a seat on the floor beside Lottie in her playroom. She was surrounded by teddy bears—most in Railers sweaters—and one lop-eared stuffed rabbit she'd named Patty. The tiny table was set for a tea party, and my princess was wearing a pale blue sparkly gown, with yellow wool socks and a tiara made of Siberian roe deer antlers. Her Uncle Stan had brought it back from his last trip to Russia. And by last, I mean final. Long story there, but yeah, she was ready for tea.

"Why?" she asked, pouring grape juice into a tiny

plastic teacup. Most of it went into the cup, so stick taps to the improvement in her pouring skills.

"Well, because we think you should listen to things other than 'Baby Shark,'" I replied, trying to wedge my legs under the table. Sitting on the little pink plastic chairs had been a hard fail.

"I like 'Baby Shark,'" she informed me.

Yeah, we knew she did. Jared was on the verge of tears last week after the bouncy little kids' song had been played at least ten thousand times in a single day. He was looking into calling the folks over at Guinness to see if that was a world record.

"Sure, yeah, Dad and I do too, but it's good to learn new songs." She studied me intently, then gave me a regal nod. "Awesome. So, here are a few tunes for a smart, pretty, princess—"

"I'm a warrior princess."

"Oh, sure, my bad. Here are some songs for a smart, pretty, warrior princess to know." I placed my cell on the table next to the peanut butter and honey sandwiches that Jared had prepared for us. He was late for tea. Charlotte, the Warrior Princess, would get cross soon. I cranked up a nice little playlist that had lots of good bands. Kids had to be taught early after all. "Birdhouse in Your Soul" by They Might Be Giants began playing.

She poured another cup of juice, then stared right at me. "Where is Daddy?"

"Oh, he's talking to Ryker," I said, wishing we still had our cushy pillows. They'd met a tragic end last week when our chocolate Lab puppy, Gordie, had torn them to shreds. Good old Borque, my brother's elderly Lab, had sired his last litter before retiring from the stud business to lie in the sun and get chubby. A fitting retirement. I hoped to do the same in about ten years. I was already thirty, so ten more years in the game might sometimes sound too short, and then, on the days when the headaches hit me or a bruising defenseman knocked me into the boards, it seemed way too far away.

"Uncle Ryker and Uncle Jab coming for Christmas?"

"I don't know, Peanut. They have a ranch now, and Ryker is playing hockey like Daddy and Dad. We'll keep our fingers crossed."

She heaved a worldly sigh way beyond her three and a half years. Then, she crossed her fingers. And her toes. Which she was showing me were crossed inside her socks when Jared finally arrived for tea, with Gordie. The pup was enthusiastic to say the least. He adored Charlotte, and she him, but his energy level was off the charts.

"Sorry to be late, your highness," Jared said, then executed a courtly bow as Gordie made a lunge for the sandwiches, nearly toppling the whole shebang. The dog was nothing if not a fool for food. Which made training easy. Our poor nanny was about frazzled. After getting the pup to sit—which was just his ass barely on the floor, tail wagging gleefully as he tried to get the peanut butter off the roof of his mouth—Jared rolled his eyes, then scanned for somewhere to sit.

"Why have we not replaced the tea pillows?" he enquired.

"No one has been to Target yet," I informed him.

"Ah. Wonderful. I love sitting on the floor for tea."

He didn't. The old goat was finding it harder and harder to get up every passing year. Thankfully, he still rose quickly in other positions. I was still feeling some intimate twinges from our lovemaking last night. Yeah, the tea pillows would have been *really* nice though.

"Dad and Daddy, I has a royal prock-a-may-shun to make," Charlotte announced after pouring some juice into a cup, then placing it on the floor for Gordie. He lapped it up, dribbling purple droplets all over the rose-colored carpet. Good thing we'd invested in that carpet cleaner.

"If it's the pony proclamation… Ugh, cripes this floor is low," Jared grunted as he lowered himself down.

I patted his thigh when he was seated. "We'll buy one of those lift chairs for teatime just for you," I teased.

He shot me a dirty look that made me snort into my tea. "You're such a wisenheimer," he tossed back as he tried to wriggle in reverse—far enough to reach the table, yet still have his spine against the footboard of Lottie's bed.

"I'm just thinking of your comfort, Sir Jared of Boomerville."

"I'm not a Boomer, thank you so very much," he muttered, his blue eyes snapping with humor and a little something sassy that said he just might show me how fit he still was tonight. I'd be up for it. Days off between home games were made for playtime with Lottie and loving time with Jared.

"Excuse me, but I has words to make off-fish-shall," Charlotte informed us.

Gordie sat up, purple juice dripping from his jowls, to stare at the queen as if waiting for the decree.

"Excuse us, please, proclaim," I told her with a little bow of my head.

Jared lifted his teacup to his lips.

"I want a brother." Grape juice flew across the table, Jared doing a spit-take Gene Wilder would've envied. Gordie leapt up to lick up the juice. Sandwiches flew everywhere, juice spilled from the pot to my lap, and her royal highness had a regal meltdown.

An hour later, after Lottie and Gordie were napping on the sofa, and we'd shampooed the rug in her room, Jared and I were in the kitchen enjoying some real tea. He'd been on this honey chamomile tea kick as of late, hoping that cutting out caffeine would help him sleep better. So far robust sex seemed to do it, but it had only been a few days.

"So, where do we think she got on the brother kick?" Jared asked as he stirred some of the honey that Adler'd brought us into his mug. Ad had taken up beekeeping. Why? Not a clue, but we all suspected that it was so he could brag about having a big stinger in the locker room. They'd found out Layton was allergic, so he watched the bees from a distance.

"Probably at the indoor playground over in Camp Hill earlier," I said while dunking a Stella D'oro cookie into my tea. I'd have a few. Cookies were *not* recommended by the Railers nutritionist as healthy afternoon snacks. "She was playing with Michelle Khan."

"Oh, yes, Mrs. Khan just had a baby," Jared replied, then added one more dollop of honey to his mug. "A little boy."

"Yep. She was cooing and cuddling the baby until we left. She even skipped the jungle gym and slide to tickle tiny Joey's chin."

Jared's eyes flared. Lottie never passed the jungle gym and slide. *Ever.* I'd had to climb in a time or two to extract her when it was time to go. Jared—the old D-man that he was—was too burly to fit. The parents who had gotten to witness a hockey player trying to wedge his shoulders into a skinny tube with monkeys painted on the sides had found it pretty amusing. As had the local press the following day. Nothing says professionalism after just signing a new multi-million dollar contract like being photographed wriggling through the monkey tumble tube.

"That explains it," he commented as he began thumbing languidly through his daily read of *The Patriot News* online. The man looked sexy AF in those reading glasses.

"Yeah, I guess." I nibbled on my cookie, my phone showing a half-read article in *The Athletic* waiting for me to return to it. "You know we *could* consider it." That brought his gaze up from the local news. He studied me over the top of his DILF glasses. "What? It's not as if we haven't discussed having another baby. It was kind of always our plan."

"Well… yes, I know we've *discussed* it." He removed his glasses, folded them, and laid them by the cookie box. He assessed me intently. "Do you think it's something we should look at more closely?"

"Maybe?" I reached for another cookie, my sight darting from the cookie to Jared to the window where the glass was coated with a touch of frost around the edges. Fall was here, and it was glorious. We had pumpkins to carve, cider to drink, and Halloween costumes to decide on before the end of the month rolled around. "I mean she *is* here alone all the time."

"She's not alone. She has us, a nanny, and now, a dog."

"Well yeah, I don't mean like we Kevin McAllister her or anything, it's just…" I plucked the cookie from its wrap, then dunked it quickly into my tea, hurrying to get the shortbread treat to my mouth. I chewed, then swallowed. Jared sat across from me waiting patiently for me to make my point. "Okay, so, and *never* tell them—especially Brady—but having siblings to grow up with was pretty nice. Most of the time."

He smiled at me. "I know you love your brothers even when they act like bossy assholes or punch your new lover in the kisser."

I chuckled at the memory of Brady tossing the gloves with Jared when he'd stumbled in on us after we'd been sexing it up. God, what a moronic move on my older brother's part. As if I was a fine Regency lady who had been sullied by a rakish duke and needed my jerk toad of a brother to defend my honor.

"Yeah, they're my brothers, morons as they may be. Not that there is anything wrong with being an only child. And if we decide to only have Lottie, that's cool, but yeah, maybe she's lonely here in this big house with just a nanny. We travel so damn much. It might be nice to have another kid. They could entertain each other."

"Hmm. Is that what you three Rowe boys did? 'Entertain each other'?" Jared's glance was mischievous.

"Sometimes. If fighting or pranking each other all the time is considered entertaining each other, then yep, we sure did that." He chuckled warmly. "I don't know. Maybe we should bring it up for serious discussion. I'd be down with using a surrogate again, if we wanted to go that way."

He nodded slowly, but his attention had drifted. "We could adopt," he offered. I pushed the cookies aside as an unexpected rush of emotion surged through me. "Ryker and Jacob are always saying it's beyond sad how many children they see going through the system. I know they're seriously considering fostering, then adopting. Maybe, we could do that here in Harrisburg. There has to be a child out there who needs a good home."

"Yeah! I'm sure there are tons of kids who would love being here with us. Lottie would have an older brother or sister to play with instead of waiting for an infant to grow up enough to really engage with. Are you down with all of that?"

"Yes, I'm certainly willing to give it some deep thought. We could reach out to the Dauphin County Children and Youth Services to feel out what the process might entail. Then, once we have a better grasp of just what would be required of us if we go this way, we can make a more informed decision. Does that sound good to you?"

"That sounds great to me. Can you contact them now? Just to see what they say and who they direct us to? I'm sure we'll pass all the criteria. I just signed a new contract for six years that will drop eight million a year into our accounts. You make nice bank too."

"I'm sure money won't be an issue for us, or our backgrounds. We're pretty straightlaced."

"There's no time to get into trouble when you play hockey." He gave me an arched eyebrow. "Oh, well, right, some guys do find the time."

He moved forward, enough to rest his sexy forearms on the kitchen table. "I'll do a quick search and send off an email asking for information. Then we'll talk more later. No more cookies. You'll have to run from here to the Susquehanna Art Museum and back tomorrow morning to work off the whole sleeve you just polished off."

"I can't help it. I like my treats." I rose, planted my hands on the table, then leaned over it to plant a slow, wet kiss on my husband's honey-sweet lips.

That kiss might have developed into something much hotter had our daughter not come charging in with a long-legged Lab puppy bouncing by her side, both looking for a potty run. Jared grabbed Lottie, and I snagged the leash from where it hung beside the back door. The tingle of Jared's kiss was still on my lips as Gordie and I rushed out into the chilly October day.

Chapter Two

Jared

I didn't have siblings.

It wasn't for wont of trying on my mom and dad's part, but according to them, I was their miracle baby, and given I'd arrived when Mom was already forty-two and Dad nearing fifty, I was the last chance. We'd been tight. Hell, they'd been my biggest supporters as I'd grown up, Dad driving me to hockey practices at ass o'clock in the morning; Mom cheering, fundraising, and baking a million brownies for bus rides. Mom had passed a year before I was drafted, Dad seeming to wait to see me get my place in hockey before passing as well. I reckon he died of a broken heart, and I'm sure if Ten left me it'd be the same for me; although, if Lottie was still small, if she needed me, if any of our kids needed us, would I give in so easily? I never blamed my dad for his grief— I was already out in the world, and he was over seventy and so tired of life without Mom. I still wish I had the unconditional love of stupid-ass idiotic annoying siblings around me that Ten had from his family.

I was envious of their easy familiarity and their shared history, and always had been. Less so since I'd been dragged into the Rowe family fold, nevertheless, a sibling of my own would have been nice.

I'd always wanted a brother or sister for Ryker, but Casey and I were never going to work, and Ryker was our only kid. He had sisters from when Casey remarried, and they were close. I could imagine him at their weddings, at graduations, being there for them whenever they needed him.

I wanted siblings for Lottie as much as Ten did. I'd never realized it before he'd talked about it, and I was determined to push things forward. Unfortunately, sitting at my laptop ready to write an email to Dauphin County Children and Youth Services was an exercise in staring at a blank screen after a few aborted starts. I guess it didn't help that my first email started with a sentence that came over as we're gay, we're married, deal with it—probably not the best angle of attack—with attack being the operative word.

The second email didn't mention Ten and me as a couple, and the marriage was implied and apologetic. For fuck's sake!

I deleted that straight away.

So, it was all about happy balance, and this was something I didn't appear to be able to find.

A knock pulled me out of my strangled thought process, and after I called for whomever was there to come in, the door opening made me shut my laptop. What Ten and I were doing as a couple outside of being Railers was our business. I had far too many nosy people hovering in my office who'd easily put two and two together from my facial expression, which, according to Ten, was transparent; although, I think he had the best inside track to my brain of anyone.

"Coach, can we talk?"

Tanner Bonetti, or T-Bone as the team called him, was a kid fresh from the summer's draft, chosen by us in the fifth round, and given a two-way contract, working mostly at AHL level until Arvy had snapped a tendon, and suddenly, Tanner was called up to play with the big guns in the Railers. He'd performed well, still needed work on speed, blunt force, and second-guessing plays, but he was only twenty and talented, and best of all, malleable to the Railers style of play. It would be very easy for the team to fall back on Ten's skills all the time, but the team had to be robust around our star, from Stan in the pipes to this new kid with wide eyes and determination in every line of him. Only right now, he didn't look determined, he looked as if he was about to cry.

"Sure, come in."

He shut the door behind him, which wasn't ominous at all, and then took a seat facing me. I'd had all kinds of D-Men sit in my office, telling me a whole gamut of things, from the sublime to the ridiculous—one with a lizard incident, right through to another with his worries about his mom and her new boyfriend. My job wasn't merely to coach the game, but to understand how each man's mind worked, to get inside their heads and pull out the best of them.

"Is everything okay?" As I asked, I sat back in my chair, and deliberately pushed back from the desk a little, trying to appear approachable and not at all hardheaded and focused.

"It's not about me," he said instantly, and couldn't quite meet my eyes.

"Is it for a friend?" I encouraged gently. If he

wanted to talk about something *a friend* needed advice on, then that was something else I was used to. *My friend has this problem with a speeding fine. My friend can't understand why his edges need work...*

He blinked at me, then dipped his head as if he needed a moment to think. "No," he said quietly, "it's my brother."

The Bonetti siblings gave the Rowe family a good run for their money. Alfie, the oldest, was playing up in Vancouver, Levi was over in L.A., and both were exceptional forwards and making names for themselves.

"Which one?"

"Levi, my... the middle brother, he's in L.A.?"

"I know Levi." When you've married into a dynasty of skaters, you get to know others in the same situation pretty quickly, particularly if they are likened to the Rowe family in a ton of articles. I knew I was biased, but not one of the Bonetti family were as good as my Ten. *Hashtag, so biased.*

"He's uhm... he's..." Tanner's face crumpled, and I didn't know what to do as tears rolled down his cheeks. "He's..." His words were choked.

I was up and out of my chair in an instant, pulling it with me, grabbing the box of tissues I used to clean the whiteboard, and handing them to him as I settled next to him. I didn't know what to do, but I placed a hand on his arm, and he leaned toward me as if he needed to check I was there.

"It's okay," I soothed and patted his arm gently, wishing there was someone in the room who knew the best thing to say right now.

"It's not," he sobbed suddenly, and fuck, it was painful watching someone cry with such depth of emotion and pain dragged up from some deep dark place where grief lived.

"It's okay," I repeated, "I'm here, talk to me."

He took a Kleenex, blew his nose repeatedly, and then swiped at his eyes. He was wearing a training T-shirt and sweats, and he looked smaller than six-foot, all hunched up in the chair.

I thought on my feet—I knew Genevieve was here today, our team counsellor, and maybe she was better suited to helping Tanner. "I can listen if you need me to, or I can get Genevieve down if you need to—"

"He's my brother you know, he's my hero."

Okay, so this was a brother thing?

"I get that." Ten didn't like to admit it often, but he idolized Brady and Jamie, and even though they were rivals, they were brothers first. Siblings who were there for each other in good times and bad, able to form such a strong bond that together they were better than when they were apart.

"He used to train with me, you know, because Alfie was older and was drafted first round and was gone so quickly; so, it was just me and Levi for a long time, and then, he left, and it was just me, and I lost him for a while. We texted, met up, but we were apart. All three of us were apart, and they were the ones who knew the real me." He stopped again, tears collecting in his eyes, making the blue sheen fracture into tiny diamonds. "I hated being apart so much." He tore at the Kleenex, and I offered him the bin and some replacement tissues, which he took. "But we were always there for each other, you know?"

"Yes."

"He's been... he has... cancer." My stomach fell. I was so hoping this would be a sibling argument or something way less serious. "Medullary thyroid cancer, and they hope... but they won't be able to tell until... I can't... I don't..."

"I'm so sorry," I murmured.

He lifted his tear-filled gaze to me. "I don't know what to do," he said. "We talked on the phone, but I just want to... I need to..."

"Hug him?"

"Yes." He nodded. "I want to tell him that

whatever happens, that Alfie and me, we'll always have his back, and that… fuck!" He crumpled again.

This time, I sidled closer and put an arm over his shoulder. His brother had cancer, and that conjured up a million horrific thoughts. I glanced up at the schedule. We had two games away, in Boston and Dallas, but then we were over in LA, and I found a solution that made sense.

"Go home, Tanner, personal circumstances; take a week healthy scratch, meet us at the L.A. practices for the away game on the twenty-third."

"For real?" He was hopeful, yet destroyed all at the same time.

"I'll clear it. Take your stuff, get a flight to LA. Is he in L.A. still or did he go home?"

"LA—Mom and Dad flew in yesterday."

"Go, be there for him, okay? Family is everything."

He leaned into my hold briefly, as if he needed to draw strength from me, then he pushed out of the chair and extended a hand, which I shook. "Thank you, Coach."

"It's okay, we have your back. Can I ask if this is public knowledge?"

"There's a statement releasing tomorrow. It's just you for now."

"Okay, we got this. Go, be with your brother, kid."

I'd never seen anyone move so fast as he left the room and sprinted away. I sat in silence for the longest time. Ten had been devastated when Brady had retired; correspondingly, Brady and Jamie had been right there for Ten when he'd been injured. But they were brothers in the happy times like lifting the Cup, family events, christenings, weddings... life with all its difficulties. When I could pull my head out of the thinking stage, I took the time to walk up to Management, explained, reassured them I had a backup plan to put their minds at rest, took their condolences on the family's behalf, and then spoke to the head coach. He wasn't worried about me letting Tanner go, if anything, he could be removed from the tears and anguish I'd just seen and view the situation in black and white. Tanner would be no help on the ice if his head was in a bad place. That was professional hockey for you, and it is cutthroat in the chase for the Cup.

Then, I was back at my desk, staring at the photo of Ten and Lottie, and suddenly, I knew what to write to the Children and Youth Services, but before I sent it, I needed Ten to hear what I'd written. I knew he was in cooldown after practice, and I found him chatting to Adler about mice, or cats, or mice as big as cats, but when I caught his eye, he was immediately sober.

"What's wrong? Is it Lottie?"

"No, but can we talk?"

He frowned, because he knew me so well, and this needing to talk sounded serious, but he followed me back to the office and shut the door to give us privacy.

"What's wrong?" he asked.

"Nothing, I mean, everything. No, look…" Fuck, not a good way to start. "I was trying to write this email to Children and Youth Services, okay?"

His shoulders dropped where they'd been hunched with worry, and his expression relaxed. "Okay?"

"And I had all these fancy words, and I was getting defensive, expecting them to read it and dismiss us out of hand, but then Tanner was in here and…" It wasn't my place to reveal what Tanner had said, and I knew Ten would understand. "Let's just say it gave me perspective."

"Okay, now I'm confused." Ten took a chair and leaned forward. "Are you saying you're having second thoughts?" He kept his expression even, but I knew him too well, and I could see the question held a lot of weight.

"No, god no. I want it more than even before. I want Lottie to have a sibling. Look, it's easier if I read what I wrote, okay? Then you can tell me if you think I'm shooting and missing the net or something."

Ten shuffled in his chair and gave me his best serious face, brushing back his bangs so he could give me his full attention. "Go for it."

"Okay, so, dear whoever. I mean I don't have a name yet for whom to send this to, it's all generic."

"Sir and madam? Or just a hello?"

"Hello, doesn't seem very professional, but sir and madam is so old and shit," I muttered, and added in the sir/madam part anyway. "Anyway, dear sir/madam, I'm writing to arrange a meeting to discuss fostering and/or adoption. My husband and I have a daughter, Charlotte, three and a half, and we have a wonderful stable home that would welcome children to become part of our family." I cleared my throat and glanced at Ten, who nodded his approval. "We originally considered surrogacy, but my son's husband owns and runs the Mountain Vista Ranch, in Arizona, and they are registering to foster older children who haven't got a home or family to call their own." I paused again to breathe, realizing I'd read that lot without stopping and my chest was tight. "My husband and I have a strong marriage, constantly talking and putting our hearts into making it better daily, and we work hard in both our professional careers and in creating a home that any child would be safe in. We're specifically looking to adopt an older child, or siblings who would like to stay together, and we believe we could give them the chance of being part of a beautiful family that they could learn to love, and in return, we could love them right back. We would always be there for them, from education to careers, from play dates to relationships, and we promise to learn right alongside them. I look forward to hearing from you with a date to meet. Jared Madsen."

"Wow," Ten said.

"Is it too much? Not enough? I didn't mention our financial stability, but if they google me, and they find you, and we can prove—"

He cut me off with a kiss in a sneaky ninja move I hadn't even seen coming.

"Perfect," he whispered, and kissed me again with a soft touch of his lips to mine. "I love you, and whatever our family becomes, it will be amazing."

"I love you, too."

We hugged, and he reached over and pressed send

before I could stop him. I watched the email disappear from the screen and, suddenly, wanted to grab it back for one last spell check, but then, I don't suppose that was the important part—it was more important that they knew how much love we had to give and how desperately we wanted to make a family that mattered.

I hoped it was enough.

Chapter Three

Ten

Seriously, how damn long did it take someone to reply to an email?

It had been close to eight hours. I checked my phone again as we geared up for a game against Arizona, one of only two we'd play against the west coast team this year. Someone slapped my shoulder. I jumped, my phone bobbling out of my hand to fall between my stocking-clad feet.

"I can explain," I babbled as I knew for sure Coach had just caught me on my phone. The man hated cellphones in his locker rooms.

"Are you looking for holiday pumpkin recipes?" Stan asked as he lowered his lanky frame down beside me. "I am making pumpkin soup for party this year. Also, am dressing in super surprise mode." He nodded sharply; his gray eyes mirthful.

"You coming as fifties Elvis, sixties Elvis, or seventies Elvis?" I asked as I hurried to tuck my phone back into my locker.

"Ha! Bigly surprise for you! I am not coming as Elvis this year." I gaped at my best friend. "Is true. I am coming as Priscilla and Erik is the King."

"Wow," I murmured, trying to picture Stan in a bouffant wig. I bet he could pull it off. "So, Erik is doing Elvis."

"Yes. He is most excited and has been practicing his shaky hips dance. Why are you making romance with disaster on phone before game?"

I glanced around. Everyone was busy suiting up. Adler was way across the room reading a book about bees. If you wanted to keep something a secret you did not tell Adler. His mouth ran at warp ten.

"Okay, I'll tell you, but you have to keep a lid on it."

He stared at me blankly. "Why am I lidding it? Will it make leaks?"

"No, it's a saying. Don't tell anyone yet because it's just a maybe at this point."

Understanding dawned on his face. "Ah! Yes. Is

secret news. Oh! Did you find out that there is a secret panel in your house that leads to magical animated place with singing men and big yellow submarines?"

"I… what? No, no secret doors. Did you watch *Yellow Submarine* last night?"

"I did! Is mostly very good but confusing. Erik says it would make more sense after eating a mushroom so I order pizza in with mushroom but there is no growing of understanding."

"Yeah, I'm thinking he meant a different kind of mushroom, buddy." I clapped his thick thigh then leaned in. He did the same. "This is top secret."

"Da. Yes. Lips are zipping shut." He made the zipping-his-lips motion.

"Cool. Right, so Jared and I are looking into possibly fostering and then adopting another child."

His smoky eyes widened. Then he gave me a bear hug so powerful it drove the air from my lungs with big hearty slaps that really kind of hurt. I may have grunted as Adler's head whipped up, and he zeroed in on me.

"What's going on over there?" Adler shouted. All eyes flew to Stan and I hugging it out. "Did you hear anything about T-Bone's brother?"

"No, nothing yet." I peeled myself out of Stan's

grip, gave him a firm don't-say-a-word stare. Everyone sighed then went back to reading about bees or dressing or slapping each other with wet towels.

"I am most joyous for you," Stan whispered. Luca Reynolds, the other half of our first line defense, working with Arvy, gave me a funny look from a few feet away. Ugh, such a nosy bunch. "As you know I am big subscribing to the more children and dogs in a house the happiest the pot of potato and leek soup is!"

"Thanks," I said as I tried to make the jump from kids and dogs to pots of soup. I gave up after a minute. Best not to overthink some things my bestie said when excited. "But it's just an idea yet. They might not want a gay couple to adopt an older child."

"Pash!" He waved a gigantic hand in my face. "Being gay is good for adopting! Is making diverse parents for happy children. I will speak for your behalf if they say being gay parents is not good. I am good for speaking. They will listen. If they do not, I will convince them. I know people."

"Oh hey, wow, thanks for the offer but I'm sure it'll all be good. I'm just stressing it. Oh wow, man, look at the time!" I pointed at the clock over the doorway. "You better get your goalie head on."

"Ah yes, I am going now to gird loins and find

goalie head." He stood, bent down, kissed my head, and wandered back to his side of the locker room. Luca was staring at me with a wrinkled brow.

I ignored Luca and suited up, eager to hit the ice and work off some of this nervous energy. Knowing we were facing off against the Raptors always brought out the best in us. Arizona had slogged hard to become a genuine contender of a team. They had some great goaltending with Colorado Penn in the net, and their forwards were led by Tate Collins. Their defense was now scary big and strong, led by Vladislav Novikov, aka The Iceberg.

Tate and I had some history—both of us had played for Dallas before coming to our respective teams. I knew him pretty well. I also knew Penn well. We'd roomed together during the last Olympics, and he'd shown himself to be way deeper a human being than I'd assumed he was. Vlad was an icy bastard, not rude or mean, but silent. Stoic. And massive.

He and Stan were friends. There was a rather decent-sized contingent of Russian players here in the States. Most of them had been keeping their heads down as things with their country and the rest of the world were not good. I never prodded Stan about his family back home, but I knew he constantly worried over them. I studied Vlad during the anthem, rocking back and forth, pondering on how I could get his ire up without getting punched in the head.

"You wish to say something to me?" Vlad asked as he moved in for the first faceoff. I wasn't even going up against him. "I see you have been eyeballing me. Would you like to ask me out for a dinner meal perhaps?"

"I'm pretty sure our significant others might take offense at that. I was just trying to figure out if what I heard about you was true and it is. You *do* look like Squidward."

His eyebrows knotted. "I'm sure I do not."

"Oh yeah, you so totally do," Adler piped up as he skated in. "How has no one told you that before? Oh, hey, I bet it's because they didn't want to make you cry."

That one hit true. Vlad bristled and mouthed something at Adler in Russian, and then glowered at me until I turned my back to face-off against Vlad's boyfriend.

"You giving him grief already, Rowe?" Tate asked as we hunkered down.

"Just pointed out that he looked like Squidward," I replied innocently.

Tate rolled his eyes. "No, he doesn't."

"I think so. Of course, squidness is in the eye of the beholder."

"If you two are done talking about the inhabitants of Bikini Bottom, can we possibly get on with the game?" the ref asked, with a little smile tugging at his mouth.

I was about to reply when Adler's voice bounced over us.

"… just saying that if you wanted to quit hockey to be a cartoon character you could," Adler was shouting over the roar of the fans.

"Shut up, Lockhart. Your face is a cartoon, and your voice is stupid. Also, I think you are so dumb that most cartoons for children go zooming over your head," Vlad fired back.

"Oh yeah? I bet I know more about *SpongeBob* than you do."

"You know *nothing* of *SpongeBob*!"

The ref threw a scowl at the two mouthing off behind me. "If I hear one more word, I'm throwing both of you out for delaying the game and making me stand here and listen to two grown men arguing over a cartoon starring a damn sponge!"

Things settled. I barely won the faceoff and the Railers barely won the game. Penn was doing gymnastics in his crease, and Stan was a brick wall.

There was a wobbly goal late in the second off the tip of my stick that somehow slithered past Colorado. Other than that, nothing really got going offensively. It was early in the season so perhaps that was why. Or maybe my mind was elsewhere. When the buzzer for the end of the third period wound up, Vlad and Adler got into a little pushing match down by Penn's net. I wasn't on the ice then, but I heard Novikov bellowing at Adler that he could sing the *SpongeBob* theme song in Russian and let's see Lockhart do that. Which Adler couldn't, so it looked like Vlad won that round of the great cartoon mind fuck game. Or had he? As we'd come away with the win I'd say the Railers won but just by the width of one of Mrs. Puff's hairs.

Seemed the email reply had gone to Jared and not me.

DOH Tennant.

A week later we were sitting in a dull office at Dauphin County Children's and Youth Services talking to a really handsome Black man who looked exhausted. I could only imagine how utterly exhausting social work was. His name was Dale Murphy, and he was sipping a cup of coffee. More than likely to keep his eyes open. We were his last clients of the day. That they'd squeezed us in so quickly probably had a lot to do with our prestige. I didn't like to name drop, nor did Jared, but sometimes it didn't hurt to mention that you had lunch with the governor at a fundraiser.

"Okay, so we'll get your background checks sent out," Dale informed us.

Jared and I were nervous as new nuns at a kegger, sitting up straight as if we were in school before the principal, our fingers meshed. Dale didn't bat an eye when he saw we were a same-sex couple. Nor did he comment on our holding hands while we chatted. Which was good because even though Jared's palm was sweaty, his touch was keeping me anchored. ·

"Looking over all the financial records I'm going to say that won't be an issue at all. The only things that might concern us is that you both seem to travel a great deal and that Mr. Rowe has an ongoing medical condition that seems to affect his mental well-being?"

Shit. I threw a fast look at Jared. His lips flattened.

"Uhm that's really not exactly as bad as it sounds on paper," I rushed to explain. "Do you follow hockey?" Dale shook his head. "Okay, that's cool. A few years ago, I was hurt while on the ice and suffered a pretty severe head injury. I did the rehab and am now playing with little to no side effects on the ice. Occasionally, I get migraines that put me down for a few hours." Or a day, but I wasn't going to say that and scare the guy. "I have meds and they help. It's called chronic post-concussive headaches or migraines. As far as we know there is no link between the headaches and CTE in my case, but we keep testing regularly and I show no other signs of chronic traumatic encephalopathy."

There. It was out. No way could I have hidden that nor should I.

"I'm sorry to hear that," Dale said, his brown eyes sad. "One of my favorite football players was knocked out just last week with a concussion. Pretty bad ·one. Would you object to us gaining access to your medical records?"

"Nope. Reach out to the team. They've been made aware that we were going to start this process," Jared piped up, knowing that talking about my brain stuff made me tense. It was a fear I lived with. Something I shoved it into a mason jar and buried it in my mental backyard. I knew the jar was there, hidden beneath the soil, but it was out of sight. Out of sight meant out of mind. And most days I could pretend that concern wasn't resting in my brain garden. Some days, when the headaches roared to life, that jar of worry was a lot harder to ignore. Still, it was the price I willingly paid to play the game I loved.

"Thank you. Your cooperation will make the process easier. So, are you looking to take in an older child? Please say yes."

"Yes, we are," Jared and I replied in unison.

That got us a bright smile from Dale.

"That's wonderful to hear. We have so many kids who are older and will cycle out of the system. Your family profile seems in order. As soon as we get the go ahead from the criminal and child abuse clearances and have your medical records in hand, we should be able to start things. We'll then do a home study. What you'll be expected to do is take part in our parent preparation courses. We'd like to see you both get twenty-four hours logged but that's not a steadfast rule. We'll work those sessions around your schedules, of course. What age and sex are you thinking of for your next child?"

Jared and I exchange an amused look. "Our daughter has already said she wants a brother. Perhaps a younger child. Say under ten. Race is not a factor," Jared said.

"Or is sexual identity," I hurried to tack on. I knew that some kids as young as four or five knew they were not happy in their body so we would be totally welcoming to any child who was trans or non-binary or any beautiful shade of queer.

"Good, good. That will help us a great deal. You'll be besieged with all sorts of information and forms. Don't let that rattle you. Decide if you'd like to foster then adopt or just adopt a child in the system. Once you have that decision made, you'll be able to browse an adoption and permanency website where you can view information on some of the wonderful kids who are looking for homes."

"Thank you," I said, sensing Dale was ready to call this meeting to a close and go home. We all rose and shook hands. The outer office was quiet when we left with a folder packed full of papers and forms.

Jared glanced at me as we made our way to the elevator. "You're awfully quiet. Are you having second thoughts? We can postpone this if you're feeling anxious."

"No, I'm fine." I rubbed the nape of my neck.

"Headache?" The elevator pinged, the door sliding open. We entered the empty elevator then Jared poked the *G* button.

"Not really. Just worry I think. He looked pretty suspicious about my head. What if my medical shit bars us from taking a new child into our home?"

"Then we go the private adoption route. Or we use a surrogate again." He reached out to give my cheek a soft caress. "There are lots of routes for us to take. I have a good feeling though. People have lots of medical conditions, Ten."

"Well sure, but this isn't hypertension we're talking about here. We don't know that I won't act out in ten or fifteen years. What if I act all aggressive or—"

He cupped the back of my head and kissed me into silence. Just a short peck, soft as down, but it was enough to stop the rumble of worry that had been building. I sighed, let my eyes close, and drew in the aroma of man and cologne. It was his unique scent and it always calmed me.

"Thanks," I whispered.

He brushed his lips over mine again then stepped back. My eyes opened slowly as the elevator touched down on the ground floor.

"Everything will be fine. Have faith. Now let's go home and spend the night with Lottie. Tomorrow is the start of that Canadian road trip."

"Poutine. My one weakness."

"I thought that was me?"

Yeah, okay, he was right. Fries with brown gravy and cheese curds came second to this man.

But it was a close second.

Chapter Four

Jared

Whoever thought it was a good idea to send us to LA, then back up to Seattle after our short Canadian road trip needed their brains checked. Somehow, we hadn't gotten things right; we lost against Calgary, a bad loss of four goals to freaking nothing, and then it was a late deflection from Adler's head onto Ten's stick in overtime that got us a shaky win in Toronto.

And now LA, with the mood in the plane reflective, and yet more traveling where it was impossible not to dissect the games and work out where we'd fucked up against two teams that shouldn't have been so hard to beat. It didn't matter whether we lost by five or won by a single goal, it was still the points that mattered, and out of a possible four points we took a poor two, and Washington were right on our tails in the rankings. Coach Benning called it a blip, a minor issue, something none of us needed to address in a major way. Adler might have saved our skin, but he'd been playing sloppily until then, Ten was looking tired, Stan had taken the first loss bad and was in a mood from hell, and Bryan, who was in net for the second game, seemed utterly miserable. It didn't sit right when our tendies weren't in a good headspace but add in other niggles and I was feeling out of sorts.

Or maybe it was because we were heading back to L.A. and Tanner was rejoining the team. He'd texted me twice, both times to thank me for letting him go home and asking me questions I didn't know how to answer. Would the Railers trade him to L.A. if they could offer something in return? Should he leave the game altogether if his brother didn't rally from the operation?

How could I answer those questions? Teams didn't just go into trades because players asked for them, and black and white Management would want a good return for losing Tanner, and there was no one on the L.A. defense I would pick out of a lineup who could slot into Tanner's space. He was a second line defenseman and a damn good one, and it would be a loss to the D-pair if he left. I didn't want to move Luca and Arvy from first line, and Westy missed Tanner from his side on the second line—James 'Westy' Sato-West was a creature of habit, and he hadn't gelled with the kid up from our feeder team.

It was a mess, and the defense was exactly where the team were struggling right now. Hell, there was only so much the forwards could do to take charge of the game without a solid defense in front of our net.

Someone sat next to me and hopes that Ten has made his way to the front to chat were dashed when it was Mac who took the seat.

"Coach," he began carefully, "have you heard anything from Tanner? About his brother? Is everything okay?"

He was holding his cell phone, twisting it in his hands, and I knew Westy and Tanner were friends, and he'd probably been hoping to hear from Tanner.

"I don't have any news."

"I don't want to just land at Tanner's side and have nothing to say to him. He needs me to be strong and shit, and fuck, I know his brother from family barbecues, we've played poker, he's a good guy. He's my same age and yet he's facing…" Westy shook his head. "And then he's not answered my texts and I have nothing I can say to him. I've sent stuff, like I'm here for him, and if he needs me, but why would he need me? We just play hockey together. Shit." He scrubbed at his eyes, his phone bumping his nose. A creature of habit, I knew Westy missed Tanner badly, but I had nothing to reassure him with.

"He'll be at practice, and you know what he'll want more than anything?"

Westy seemed hopeful. "What?"

"Normality. He'll probably want to play hockey and forget everything when he can."

"You think?"

I was a coach, and sometimes that meant I couldn't be a friend, and I wanted to say hockey was the one thing that helped me to find some peace when Ten was in the hospital. I didn't say any of that because it was personal to me and Ten, and the team had to be kept separate with some things.

Still, I could reassure him with confidence. "I don't think, I know." I could've been lying, but Westy nodded and then gave me an uncertain smile.

He was built like a giant, six-four, strong, fast, formidable on the ice, but right now he looked vulnerable and sad. There was only so much a coach could do, but I hoped I'd done enough for now, without doing very much at all.

"You're in my seat, kid," Coach Gagnon muttered.

Westy immediately got up and headed back to the team.

"It's not your seat," I reminded our goalie coach.

"It is now." He sat next to me and opened his iPad.

I groaned—he had X's and O's and copious notes as he flicked through. So much for an hour or two of quiet fretting about Tanner, and the adoption process, and the team's two-game slump—it seems like we were working.

"Westy needs to know that…"

We landed a little after midnight, and the bus took us directly to the hotel near the arena. Our room allocations dealt with quickly and efficiently and Ten and I shared a room on all road trips. Once they'd tried to separate us—Ten played so shit the next game the powers that be changed their minds sharpish. Sure, there were times we were apart, like the Olympics, and the time he'd gone home for a quick visit with his parents, but they were few and far between.

He closed the door, and then it was us hiding

away from the world. I tugged him into a hug and held him tight, breathing in the scent of him, my stubble catching on the collar of his pristine shirt, and his kiss to my forehead gently encouraging.

"Did we hear something about the adoption?" he asked cautiously. "Or have you got news about T-Bone's brother?"

"Nothing from the agency, but Tanner's coming to practice in the a.m."

There wasn't much planned for tomorrow's practice—it would start later given how late we'd flown in, and it would be about stretching and casual skating more than anything else. I wanted to get Tanner and Westy back together, but as a precaution our call-up from the feeder team, Reuben, had come with us—in case Tanner wasn't in a good headspace. Sometimes I hated the business decisions we had to make in such a fluid situation where it was all grays.

"It will be good to see him." He flicked through some pictures of Lottie sent to us by her doting grandma who was back at our house to *help* the nanny. We all knew it was her way of spending time with her granddaughter, but neither of us said it. We smiled at the photos, made the usual parent comments about how beautiful our baby was, and then stopped when I yawned widely.

"Getting tired, old man?" Ten joked.

He encouraged me to shrug off my suit jacket, and helped me out of my pants and shirt, then asked me to lie back on the bed before tugging off my socks and stripping himself. I must have been tired because all I wanted was a hug—a really close, and forever kind of hug, and Ten knew me better than he knew himself. We took it in turns to use the bathroom and then snuggled under the covers.

I rested my head on the soft downy pillows. "I'm not old," I defended as if I'd only that moment thought of it.

"Nope, you're the perfect age for me," Ten murmured. "You always will be."

"I hope we get good news."

"About the adoption or about Tanner's brother?"

"Both, but I hope that the op was a success for Levi, and they pulled out every fucking cell of that cancer and that he'll be okay."

"Me too."

He kissed my cheek and sighed as he tenderly smoothed his hand over my skin. "I saw Mac came up to see you."

"He's all over the place missing Tanner."

Ten sighed. "And worrying about Levi, I bet."

"Mostly about Tanner, but what do you mean about Levi?"

"I've seen them together, Westy and Levi, I mean, and there's tension. You know? Westy and Tanner might be best friends but it's Westy and Tanner's brother Levi with the sparks."

I certainly didn't know, but then the last time we'd partied with the L.A. team had been a few years back when we'd played them just before Labor Day. Their team captain had arranged a barbecue—that much I recalled—but I don't remember one of my D-Men being particularly interested in one of LA's forwards. Shouldn't that have hit the LGBTQ gossip chat group by now? Or had I missed it because I was hardly ever actually on there? Ten often called me oblivious to most things, including sexual tension—clearly he was right.

Ten shifted then yawned.

"Hard game," he muttered, and that was the last thing he said before he fell asleep as fast as you could say the word exhausted, soft puffs of breath against my skin, and his chest rising and falling in a familiar rhythm. I couldn't sleep at first, my head spinning with worries and concerns and Coach Gagnon and his X's and O's, Tanner, and his brother Levi, and Westy and his sexual tension with Levi. Still, Ten had me wrapped in his arms, and it was the perfect place for me.

So, I slept.

Morning practice was quiet, Tanner was back with us, but the prognosis for his brother Levi was far from certain. The surgeons had operated, but tests were still in progress, and that was all he could tell us. I liked to think Tanner was here today and losing himself in hockey, but that didn't last long when Westy cornered him, and they had a heated debate along with waving hands. So much for my D-partners gelling again because whatever Tanner said had Westy wincing, and then skating away from him with a sad shake of his head.

Fuck knows what had happened there, and I resolved to ask Ten, or maybe I should just start reading messages in our group.

Tanner assured the coaching team that he was good for tomorrow's game, and he certainly gave the impression of being focused, but none of us could make a final decision until we discussed it together. I could advise Coach Benning but in the end it was his decision.

The lone bright point happened after practice,

when all the guys headed back to the hotel, and Ten and I headed out in a cab for the Griffith Observatory. It was one of my favorite places with its views of the city, plus the history, and the hummingbirds in the bushes out front. With a cap low on Ten's head, in the hope no one recognized him in our generic T-shirts and jeans, we planned to enjoy an ambling kind of afternoon. As Ten showed me a scene from an old *Star Trek* show that had been filmed here, my cell vibrated with an incoming call. I was slow to answer, fumbling and swiping the wrong way, but it was a withheld number so it might well have been a sales call and I didn't worry about missing it.

They called back. This time we connected, and I readied my not-interested tone. Only it wasn't some random sales call, it was the department about the adoption, and the voice identified himself as Dale Murphy from Dauphin County. The chances of a match this early in the game were slim, and maybe he was just calling to check our middle names or something, but also, it could be the best news.

"Hang on, Dale, I'm taking you somewhere private." Ten's eyes widened when I used the name, and he made some complicated hand gesture I had no hope of understanding.

"No worries," Dale said.

I glanced around me, searching for an elusive place where people wouldn't be able to hear us talk.

"What does Dale want? What is he saying?" Ten mouthed.

"Nothing yet," I mouthed back.

Immediately he joined me in the search for privacy, and we finally found a shady corner in an alcove that I hoped to god had cell reception. Ten pulled out his headphones and slotted them in. We took an ear bud each.

"We're here, Ten as well, I mean," I said.

"This is complicated," Dale began, "and don't feel obligated because I know you said you were looking for one child under ten. Thing is, you indicated you were happy to take on a child who needed you and a case giving us cause for concern has crossed my desk again, and I wonder if you'd be interested."

Ten opened his mouth, probably to say yes to anything, but I pressed a finger to his lips. I wanted to give a kid a good home, but I wanted to know we could be the best for them from the start.

"Go on," I encouraged, and tried not to sound too excited.

"This is actually two children, a fourteen-year-old boy, and his nine-year-old brother. The eldest lists hockey as a hobby, and I do recall he has a stick in his room."

Two? And one much older than we expected? Was that what we wanted? Were we ready for that? Ryker had been a good teenager, one who loved hockey and had been just low-key teenage hell, but two boys in our house ruled by Lottie? Could we do that?

Ten must have realized I'd gone into panic mode, because it was he who organized things for when we got home.

Tomorrow, Dale was meeting us apparently to do the first of at least three or four home visits. As the social worker assigned to the boys, he would give us a clearer picture with all the available information: family background, including what events had led to them being on their own, or anything that might affect the boys' health. I didn't think Dale could tell us anything we couldn't handle.

Right?

And, in three days, we were meeting Soren, fourteen, and Milo, nine. Brothers, and orphaned when Soren was eight and Milo only three. They'd bounced around the system, and that was all Dale could tell us until tomorrow.

Somehow, it was all we needed to know.

Maybe they could get to us and stop moving?

Maybe *we* could offer them the perfect home.

Chapter Five

Ten

"Should I go suit or tee?" I asked, holding up a dress shirt in one hand and a Marianas Trench T-shirt in the other.

"Dress shirt," Jared said as he fiddled with a tie.

"Tee," Mom said as she tried to corral Lottie into wearing a dress, the chase around the house ending in our bedroom. "You don't want the boys to think they're meeting yet more adults in suits. Not that you don't look nice, Jared."

He sighed, untied his tie, and flung it to his dresser. "No, you're right. Casual is the way to go. Not sure how well I'd be able to carry off a rock band tee though."

"Daddy, wear the dress!" Lottie shouted as she scurried across our bed to find one of about ten discarded shirts of mine. She wiggled into an old Railers sweater. "I wearing this to meet my new brothers!"

Mom gave me a look that said she didn't think we should have told Lottie about Soren and Milo yet. I knew she'd not been in favor of Lottie knowing but we'd been so excited. And she was part of the family, a big and rather loud part, so should be included in all aspects of this adoption. If the boys didn't like a nearly four-year-old girl then we'd know right off and could move on with our search. Mom felt telling Charlotte might set her up for a disappointment.

"I don't think your dress will fit me," Jared replied then began digging into his drawers for a casual outfit.

"You loved this dress yesterday." Lottie pushed the dress away with vigor every time Mom held it up to her.

"Yesterday is in my memory now," Lottie informed us.

I chuckled while tugging my T-shirt over my head.

Mom sighed.

"She has a point," Jared remarked, holding up a

nice blue polo that set off his incredible eyes. Mom and I both bobbed our heads. "We'll save the dress for another day. Can you put leggings on under your Daddy's sweater?"

"Why?" Lottie asked, falling back onto our bed then slinging her feet into the air, showing God and the world her brand-new pink panties. So far we'd had no accidents for three whole days. Who knew what today would bring? Sometimes she held it too long if she was busy, and I suspected she would be incredibly busy charming or terrifying the boys.

"So, no one sees your underwear," Mom told her as she handed the dress to Jared and scooped up Lottie from the bed.

Lottie curled around her grandma, kissing her on the cheek. "I'm a big girl. I like people to see my panties! Then they know I'm a big girl too."

Mom looked at me. I shrugged. "You're no help at all, Tennant." She shook her head, and then took Lottie out to find leggings.

"Yikes. I got the look," I gasped then staggered over to Jared, hand on my heart. I fell into his side then clung to him. He snorted in amusement. "You look nice," I said, kissing him on his smooth cheek. "Tense but nice."

"I'm nervous. What if the boys don't like us?"

"How can they not? We're incredibly cool." I glanced in his mirror, ran my fingers through my hair, and decided I was good to go.

"No, *you're* incredibly cool. I stopped being cool when Ryker was about thirteen. Ask him. He'll verify it."

"I *am* pretty damn cool." I gave him a wink. "You'll be fine. You know what makes us work so well?"

"I suspect I'll regret this but tell me," he replied as his arms slipped around my waist.

"The combination of big-Dad feels you throw off mixed with the funky down-with-everything vibes I have."

"I'm pretty sure the kids aren't saying 'funky' anymore."

"I'm bringing it back. You look fine. Come on, let's get our daughter and go meet our possible future sons." I offered him my hand.

He took it but he looked ready to remind me to not count chickens before they hatch. Which I totally was not doing. Not really. Okay, yeah, I was totally counting chicks. Hopefully that didn't spin around and peck me on the ass.

· · ·

We were late arriving at Wildwood Park. It'd taken us longer than it should have to get one preschooler and one puppy into the car. Mom had asked if we were sure we wanted to hit the boys with a rowdy little girl and a rambunctious Lab. If they were coming into the family—maybe—they might as well get the whole chaotic mess at once. Besides, who didn't love perky girls in lime-green leggings, purple sneakers, and a Railers jersey down to her toes? And puppies? I mean, seriously, who didn't love dogs?

"Okay, so maybe your mother was right," Jared huffed as we raced through the park, Lottie pulling on me to go one way, Gordie pulling on Jared to go another.

"Nah, we got this." I hefted the important-shit-we-need-to-carry-around-with-us bag higher on my left shoulder, then swept Lottie off her feet and deposited her on my right hip. She giggled merrily as I broke into a jog, heading with all due speed toward the nature center where we were meeting Dale and the boys.

The park was a favorite place of ours. Filled with hiking trails, trees, and marshlands, there was wildlife everywhere, from herons to turtles basking in the sun, to an enormous variety of songbirds and waterfowl.

Lottie loved the turtles the best and was already complaining when we didn't break off onto one trail to visit them.

"Gordie, no, stop smelling that. No, that is—drop that!" I heard Jared correcting the pup behind me.

"Gordie being bad," Lottie informed me as we hustled along.

We'd just made it to the nature center, the summer coneflowers now having died off and replaced with mums. Leaves were already falling to the ground, the bright reds and yellows blanketing the walkways.

"Hey, Tennant!" a man called. I skidded to a halt, hoping it wasn't a fan. Not that I didn't love our fans, I did, but I was kind of hoping to keep the whole "Generational Superstar" thing tamped down a bit. It could be a lot. And while it might seem cool at first for older kids it would probably get embarrassing fast. Glancing to the left, I saw Dale rising from a bench. There were two young men with him, both looking a little leaner than my mother would like. Dark hair much like mine, and dark brown eyes unlike mine or Jared's. Soren, the eldest, got to his feet instantly, sliding in front of his younger brother in a blatantly protective move. Milo, the youngest, peeked around his brother, cautious, until he saw Gordie.

Then he burst free of Soren's hold and dashed to

the Lab with a squeal. Gordie was all about kids. And kisses. The two of them fell to the leafy walkway, Milo giggling madly as Gordie cleaned his face for him. Jared hurried into the fracas to unwind the leash from around Milo then try to get the pup back under control. Soren walked over to his brother, gathered him up, brushed him off, and then stood silently staring up at me.

"What a greeting," Dale laughed, coming around the two boys to shake our hands. "As you can see, the boys love dogs."

"And our dog loves them," Jared said as Gordie sat beside him. Well, sit was a stretch. His backside was barely touching the ground. His wagging tail seemed to lift his butt skyward. "It's a pleasure to meet you both. I'm Jared, and this is Tennant." I took off my cap, then plunked it onto Milo's head.

He grinned up at me.

"Daddy, tell my brothers who me is!" Lottie demanded.

"Sorry, this is our daughter, Charlotte," Jared said.

"Puts me down," Lottie said.

I did as she asked. She paraded right up to Soren, he of the wary eyes and sullen face. She shoved her hand out to him.

He glanced at me, hesitation and distrust in his eyes.

"Shake my hand, please," Lottie told him.

He glanced at Dale, then at Jared, that tension still in place, then he looked down at Lottie. A bit of the unease evaporated. He took her tiny hand. She was barely up to his hip. Soren was a gangly kid. All arms and legs as young guys were, his guard up, which we'd been told to expect. Kids in the system for a long time tended to not trust easily.

"I am your sister."

"Lottie, they're not your brothers yet," Jared hurried to explain.

"I'll be your brother," Milo spoke up, shook her hand, and then stood there staring at us, Lottie's fingers meshed with his.

"Okay, Daddy, he's my brother now. He said so," Lottie announced to the world easy as you please. We all chuckled, aside from Soren. He wasn't going to be charmed by a cheeky girl in a jersey forty-eight times too big for her. "You can be too. Come with me." Lottie held out her other hand to Soren. His sight flickered to Dale. Dale gave him a whatever-you-want-to-do-dude sort of shrug. "Come with me. I know where the turtles live."

Soren, obviously a smart young man, took Lottie's

hand. Off she stomped, pulling the boys along behind her, mouth going a mile a minute.

"Well, there's that," Dale joked.

Gordie yanked on his leash to follow the kids so we fell in behind the trio, talking to the boys as best we could from the rear. We took a nice nature hike, easing up to stroll along beside the threesome.

"Do you guys like being outside?" I asked as we lingered by a turtle pond. Tiny box turtles were lined up on a mossy log sunning themselves.

"I like to hopscotch," Lottie informed me.

"Yeah, I know, sugar, I was asking the boys," I told her. She pulled a perfect moue. "Do you boys like to play outside? Do you do any sports?"

I knew Soren played hockey, that was in his bio, but I wanted to get the young man to speak to us. He'd conversed with Lottie, who I had to assume he felt was safe, but he'd not said a word to Jared or myself. Milo seemed less closed off, easier to engage, and, of course, was enchanted with Gordie.

"I play skateboards," Milo informed me, tossing his bangs from his face. His jacket was a size too big, his pants as well, but he seemed at ease in them. I'd been the same way as a kid. Had no cares about clothes or how they fit as long as my backside was covered.

"You *ride* skateboards," Soren gently corrected, his sight on the turtles' shiny shells. A mallard duck and his mate swam past. Gordie, true to his breed, insisted on fetching the ducks. Jared was on the ball though and prevented a puppy-in-the-pond moment. That made the boys laugh. Both of them. Soren gave me a sideways appraisal after the ducks were gone. "I used to play hockey."

"Oh, why did you stop?" I asked, prodding him a bit since he was at least talking.

"The last place we were at, they had some money. This place they don't." He glanced back at the turtles.

"Yeah, hockey is expensive," I confessed. That was no lie. How my folks ever afforded to put three kids through the sport, I had no clue. "Maybe we could get you hooked up with the Railers youth hockey program. Then you could play and not have to worry about the cost of equipment."

He threw me a look that was so close to a dare I felt the jab in my gut. "Whatever."

Ouch. I glanced at Jared. He raised a shoulder. I had no idea how to recover from that cold shoulder, so I just fumbled into something else, asking Milo if he had ever been to the reptile farm outside the city. He said he hadn't, but he was keen to go. Lottie was a seasoned vet out at the farm and had her own season pass. Grandma and her nanny took her whenever they could, which proved how much my mother adored her because Mom was terrified of snakes.

"Cool, maybe we can do the reptile farm next time and then have some dinner?" I asked nonchalantly while Gordie sniffled along the edge of the pond, blowing bubbles in the brackish water, which got a giggle from all the kids. Even Soren.

"Yeah!" Milo and Lottie shouted, putting the mallards to wing.

"'Next time'?" Soren sounded shocked—as if he wasn't sure he'd heard correctly.

I glanced to Jared, who nodded. The meeting had been a good one, all things considered. We'd not expected to have the boys fall in love with us right off the bat, especially the older one who had been shuffled from one home to another for so long.

"If that's okay?" I glanced from Soren to Dale.

"It's fine with me. What do you say, guys?"

Both boys agreed. Milo enthusiastically and Soren… well, he agreed.

"We'll set it up before we leave. How about in a week or two?" Dale asked while rubbing Milo's shoulder affectionately.

"Tomorrow?" Milo asked.

"Yes, tomorrow! Gammy comes too. She makes

faces at the snakes like this." Lottie pulled out a comical, exaggerated look of terror that had all of us laughing. Soren didn't bust a gut, but he *did* smile. Well, he did before he clocked me watching him then he wiped the smile immediately.

"Let's see what our schedules say," Jared interjected, leading the dog from the pond.

We all fell in line then, making small talk about skateboards, lizards, the pretty trees, and the way the wind smelled like pond water when it blew into our faces.

When we got back to the parking lot, we got the kids and dog into our respective vehicles, then pulled out our phones. Aligning schedules was tricky. We had games every other night and skates every morning. This homestand was a long one thankfully, and we finally managed to wiggle in the reptile farm and dinner for the upcoming Friday afternoon. We'd make sure it was an early night as we had an afternoon game that following Saturday against Boston. One did not go up against Boston half asleep. Though they'd been through some hard times recently, I never counted them down for long. Brady's determination and grit still lingered in that club, despite the fact my brother was no longer on the ice.

"Oh hey," I said as we were getting ready to go. "I

have stuff for the guys in the back of the car." I jogged around the back, opened the hatch, shoved the diaper bag aside, and yanked out a Railers duffel bag. I'd signed and stuffed all kinds of things into it. Jerseys, ball caps, mittens, beanies, a stuffed bear in a Railers sweater, a couple of calendars. I picked up the stick I'd autographed as well. I glanced over my shoulder at Jared, giving him a should-I-or-shouldn't-I? look as I held the stick.

He nodded once, then handed Lottie a granola bar that Gordie tried to intercept.

Tugging it all free, I then padded around the sedan that Dale drove and rapped on the back window. Soren stared at me through the glass, his brown eyes showing zero emotion. I held up the duffel and the stick. That made his eyes widen even if only for a second. The window slowly went down.

"This is for you and Milo. Just some stuff. The stick is one that I used last year in a playoff game against Washington. It was set aside for a raffle, but I have tons. Thought you might like it, you know, if you can get back on the ice."

He gawked at me. I had to think he was trying to gauge how much he should display in terms of excitement. His mouth might be set but his eyes were dancing. I just hung around as he worked things out, stick in one hand, duffel in the other, chilling. Finally, he held up his hand. I passed over the stick then the duffel. Milo dug into it instantly, finding mittens he pulled on although it wasn't mitten weather yet. His smile was bright as the fall sun overhead.

"Thanks," Soren said softly, angling the stick through the window and over his lap.

"You bet. See you Friday." I rapped the roof of the car. The window went back up, cutting off Milo's gush over the goodies in the bag. "Thanks for the outing," I called to Dale resting against the fender of his car as he typed away on his phone.

"Thank *you*," Dale replied, pocketed the cell, and slid behind the wheel.

Off they went, back to another foster home where, I hoped, the people were kind to them. Sadness washed over me. I couldn't imagine what those two had been through. Losing their parents, then being moved from one place to another for years and years. My childhood had been pretty ideal. Solid home, loving parents, always enough food, money for hockey for three kids. We'd never been hungry, or scared of being alone, or dirty. Well, that was a lie. We were dirty a lot, but that was our own choice. Milo and Soren had nothing but each other. Maybe, if we were lucky, Jared and I could change that. Every kid deserved adults who loved them. And a pushy little sister. And a dog to whisper secrets to.

I heard Lottie giggling over the fact that the dog was licking her toes.

Toes? Where had her sneakers gone?

Chapter Six

Jared

Our game against Washington was a shit show. We'd had a comfortable win against Buffalo at home, full attendance from screaming, shouting fans, and we were high on the fact we kept the momentum going.

Only the Washington captain, Ivan Ponomarev, was having the night of his life and got two goals past Stan in the first five minutes. Ivan gloated hard over beating his fellow Russian, and to say Stan wasn't a happy camper was an understatement. Despite Ten talking to Stan, despite Alain talking to his goalie, inevitably, Coach Benning pulled Stan after the first period and Brian had to go into the net. Thankfully, he shut the door as best he could against a dominant offense, and they got another one by him—an Ivan Ponomarev hat trick—but we didn't hit back. Losing to Washington three goals to a big fat zero, in our own barn for god's sake, was humiliating and the fans let us know exactly how they felt. I couldn't say that we played badly, but Washington appeared to have the measure of us this early in the season, and clearly all the Railers coaches needed to go back to the drawing board.

It didn't help that Tanner left the game ten minutes before the end, either. Called for hooking, holding, instigating, and seemingly every other infraction under the sun, he'd finally been taken down by Ivan in a hip check so hard I thought the Plexiglass might snap under the power of it.

First off, the chat in the locker room, where Coach Benning had very little to say. Sometimes it was the things he didn't say that resonated the most, and when I caught Connor's eye he shook his head in a subtle movement, the captain taking the weight of the loss on his shoulders. I noticed Ten had removed his jersey and was tracing the *A* on the chest, and I knew he was thinking about all the things he thought he should have done differently.

"You will fight back," Coach summarized, and the team, as one, said yes.

I followed Westy, who began pacing outside the medic's room, still in his gear, wet with sweat but with a manic gleam in his eye.

"Levi will kill me if I let Tanner get hurt!" he muttered to me, and placed a hand on the door to stop me from going in. "Tanner's losing his shit, Coach, you need to…" He closed his eyes, as if he didn't know what I should do or was reluctant to second guess me. I needed to talk to Tanner, and I glanced pointedly at Westy's hand on the door handle.

He moved it immediately. "Sorry, Coach," he muttered.

I clapped a hand on his shoulder, and he winced. "You did good tonight, James," I said firmly, using his given name instead of his nickname. "Get a shower, get some sleep. I've got this."

Westy winced, and then nodded, before dragging his exhausted self to the locker room and showers. Inside the medic's room, Tanner looked like hell, his gear off, sitting in boxers. It seemed every part of him was red and there was a nasty cut under his left eye. "Coach," he acknowledged miserably.

I glanced at our team medic, who gave me a nod. "Concussion protocol was cleared," he advised, and then busied himself down at the end of the long narrow room to give me time with Tanner. I hadn't seen a hit to Tanner's head in the game, but concussion was something no medic ignored.

"You said you'd—"

"It won't happen again, Coach," Tanner interrupted me, and I stopped talking and waited for him to explain his mindset so we could start a meaningful dialog that wasn't all macho posturing. He stared at me, I stared back, and then his gaze shifted from mine, and he slumped. "Shit," he muttered.

"We're benching you for the Boston game."

"What? No. I need to play. I have nothing else that… please… this is…" Whatever he saw in my steady gaze, it was enough for him to subside. "Yes, Coach," he finished, then tilted his chin. "I'm sorry."

I wanted to tell him he didn't need to be sorry with me specifically, that it was the team as a whole that he'd fucked over, but I'd be lying. The loss tonight wasn't all on him, although he didn't make it any better. It wasn't on Stan who had a shaky start, nor was it on Ten not scoring; it was a mess of things. Not least of which Washington had found their legs early in the season and played like it was a Stanley Cup game seven.

"Take the time to check in on your brother. You'll have mandatory time with the team counselor, be at practice tomorrow, and then suit and tie in the box for when Boston is in the barn."

He sighed heavily. Being a healthy scratch and made to sit in the box was shit, and I knew, because I'd been there in my career. Still, I reasoned he didn't fuck up tonight because he wanted out of the team. He *needed* the team, but his head was filled with things that made him step straight into chaos. I went to the door, but his soft voice stopped me.

"Levi's not looking good," he murmured.

I took a moment before facing him. "Your brother is a strong, young, man. He has every chance, Tanner."

Tanner nodded, and then slid off the table and reached for a shirt. He didn't say anything else, and I think he was done with the game, and me, and everything else, for now.

"If ever you need to talk…"

"I know, Coach."

But his tone was dead, and I wondered if maybe I was the last person he'd want to talk to.

So, with a loss to our biggest rivals, a Boston game around the corner, and Tanner sitting in the medic's room covered in bruises, I wasn't getting out of the barn before midnight, so Ten reluctantly went home. Despite how much I wanted him to stay.

By the time I joined him, it was really late and the only one awake to greet me was Gordie with his beaten-up toy rabbit in his mouth and his tail wagging so hard he was wobbling. I played with his manic self for five minutes in a random game of hallway fetch and smiled when he collapsed in a puppy heap of exhaustion on his bed in the kitchen. Then it was off to find Ten, but given the game we'd had, I knew where he'd be—asleep on the sofa. Lottie was on his chest, her fingers curled into his shirt. I gently eased her away, and she didn't even wake up as I tucked her into her bed and kissed her forehead. Next up I kissed Ten awake and then helped him up off the sofa. He wasn't entirely conscious, and I ended up tucking him in as well, but he tugged me down with him, still in my suit, and pressed his face into my neck.

"That was a shit game," he murmured.

I held him close. "Yep."

"Tanner okay?"

"Mostly."

"It's fucked up," Ten added, and pressed a kiss to my skin. "We'll beat Washington next time," he said with a yawn.

"Was Lottie fretting?"

"Nah, I just needed a cuddle. She was up for it." He smiled—even though I couldn't see his face, I knew he was smiling. "Chloe went to bed, and I got my Lottie time."

Our nanny knew what it was like on the days when we came home beaten down by a loss, second-guessing everything, and had never once suggested that Lottie didn't need to be carried to the sofa for a hug, although she frowned at us sometimes. I once heard her mutter that it was only a game, but that would be heresy, so I ignored it for all her other amazing talents in keeping our little family in order. Only a game! Never.

Practice was molasses-slow, lots of cross-ice and small-area games practice, and I had to try really hard to keep my head in the game because that afternoon we were meeting up with Soren and Milo again. I didn't have to be a mind reader to know that Ten was completely focused on adopting them. Me too, because I'd already started thinking about which bedrooms in our vast home would be best for the boys. I'd settled on two rooms at the end of what Ten joked was the west wing, but which was literally just left off the main stairs. The rooms were big and airy and came with an interconnected jack-and-jill bathroom the boys could share, and both had views out over the garden and the pool and were painted in neutral colors.

I thought the boys could choose their own color schemes, and as for furniture, we should order in some beds and units. It was the mundane stuff that became exciting, like Ten and me at seven a.m. this morning, scrolling our phones to find the right mattress and snorting with laughter at some of the descriptions.

"Firm to hard, this mattress will carry you on a wave of pleasure," Ten read out, and I snorted so hard I woke Gordie, who then wanted to play fetch with one half of my favorite pair of shoes.

Work had been forgotten then, but it was right in our faces now. Tanner was here, looking brighter, and I found him chatting to Connor, the Railers captain, listening and interjecting periodically. I didn't interrupt. Connor was a leader in the locker room, and Tanner was at ease with him. I chatted to Tanner as well, but we kept it strictly hockey, although Westy was never more than a few feet away, hovering as close as he dared without it appearing weird.

It was definitely weird.

But after practice, it was heading out for Soren/Milo time. We picked up Lottie and headed for the reptile farm. We were on time, in fact we were actually early, so we hovered in the parking lot next to our SUV and waited. I was overwhelmed with excitement, nerves, and concerns, but so was Ten from the way he kept twisting his keys in his fingers.

"I like the boys," Lottie announced, to break the silence, and then screwed up her face and gave a blinding grin. "But Gammy says boys are stinky."

She wasn't wrong—spend any time in a locker room and stink is absolutely the best word to describe it, but I imagine she was talking about Ten and his brothers, Brady, and Jamie. I don't recall Ryker being particularly stinky, apart from after hockey, but then his curly hair was his pride and joy, so he showered often. Or was that his mom making him shower often? Who knew? I'd have to ask her one day.

"Not all boys are stinky," Ten reassured her, and crouched down to adjust one of her pigtails, which had slipped a little. "I bet Soren and Milo aren't stinky."

"Hmmm," she said, as if it was a big thing to think about.

She waited impatiently for Ten to fix her hair, which was difficult when she was wriggling, and then skipped off to the welcome sign, missing when Dale's car, with Soren and Milo inside, arrived and parked next to ours. For a moment I felt a twinge of embarrassment that our car was brand new—a Tennant Madsen-Rowe sponsorship deal with a local dealership, something gifted to us, and wished we'd bought an older car that didn't stand out so much. I worried we were giving too many signals that we were attempting to buy Soren and Milo's affection. They had to understand we were normal underneath the hockey, and I made a mental note to talk to Ten about that later.

Milo was out first, in a new Railers jersey with Ten's number on the back, darting past us and heading straight for Lottie who squealed in excitement. They hugged and stared at the sign with its snakes and lizards and many hideously scary things. Soren was quick to get out, and watchful of his brother, and definitely wasn't wearing any Railers merch.

"Hi, Soren," Ten began, and I added my hi.

"Hi," he replied after a moment, and then stared at his feet, his bangs falling over his eyes.

Dale stayed quiet and hovered by the car, and with a flick of his wrist, indicated he'd be staying back and just observing. Was that how this worked? What if we were bad guys who mistreated kids? Where did the trust begin for any prospective new parent?

We're not the bad guys. He probably knows that. But how does he know that?

"… Jared? What do you think?"

I snapped out of my maelstrom of conflicting thoughts and blinked at Ten. "Sorry?"

"Shall we go inside, find the café, and get a drink first?" Ten repeated.

I bobbed my head immediately. Caffeine sounded great right about now. I glanced at Soren, who stared back at me with a hint of distrust. Shit. The last thing I should do is lose track of things. He probably thought I was pissed about something.

"Sure, I know they have all kinds of drinks in there, like Coke and coffee, although do you drink coffee? Are you too young for coffee?" Shit. Shit. Shit. Now I was rambling.

Soren pulled back his thin shoulders and tilted his chin. "Look, I get you don't want me here, but you'd better pay attention to Milo and make sure it's good for him today," he snapped, and his eyes blazed with emotion.

What did I do? That wasn't respectful, right? But then, I'd fucked up in the first place, and now it was a mess.

"Sure, we will," Ten interjected, "but, dude, that wasn't cool."

Soren snorted in disdain, "Old dude is staring at me like he doesn't want me here, but where Milo goes I go, and if either of you want sunny happy perfect Milo then you get me too, or you don't get Milo at all. You hear me?" Soren was on a tear, and I didn't know what to say—all my parenting skills had escaped me.

Ten stepped between us, and placed a hand on Soren's shoulder, which he didn't shrug off, so win one for Ten. "One, Jared is not old, two, it's not cool to be impolite."

"Whatever," Soren muttered, and then there was a silence, and finally Soren added a soft sorry, but he clearly wasn't finished.

"I know he's good," Soren began, "Milo is easy and he's a kid, and I know one day he'll find a home, but until then—until he's really safe—I won't fall for your presents and your fake smiles, and you can't separate us."

Fake smiles? Was that what I was doing? And Soren really thought we just wanted Milo? Thought that anyone who saw them wanted to split them up? No fucking way, and in a rush all my parenting skills flooded back. I tenderly eased Ten to one side, and he side-eyed me with a gentle warning in his gaze.

"Milo-Soren is a package, okay?" I glanced at Ten, who nodded. "Our intention is to adopt both of you. Together." Ten smiled then—we both knew what we wanted, and the boys were it. Soren remained unconvinced, but I had an ace I could play. "Our son, Ryker Madsen-Benson, you know him?"

"Duh," Soren muttered, and then cleared his throat. "Forward, Arizona Raptors. I know him."

"Yeah, well he'd be a big brother to both of you, and our family would be Ryker, Lottie, you, and Milo. And Jacob of course. Okay?"

Wow, that was a lot to dump on him, and I waited for him to process. I didn't expect hugs or tears or for him to give me a speech back, but I liked he gave a hesitant nod before he jogged over to find his brother and Lottie. He held out his arms and Lottie clambered up to have a hug. My chest tightened with a surge of love for the two boys we wanted to adopt.

"Way to go Daddy Jared," Ten whispered, and we both glanced over at Dale who wasn't looking our way but had probably heard it all.

"Did we just fuck up?"

"Far from it," Ten reassured me, and then hand in hand we gathered up the kids and headed in for a day of snakes and lizards.

And it was the best day ever.

Chapter Seven

Ten

I gave my husband a final once-over.

"I think your beard is too long," I told him, walking to Jared to trim the long white beard he had donned. Taking a step back, I gave the beard a final look then nodded. "Perfect. You look the part."

"Do I have to go without a shirt? This feels awkward," Jared protested as I rushed to tug on the head of my Flounder costume.

"*You* feel awkward? Try bumbling along as a fish," I said from inside the cavernous yellow-and-blue felt fish head.

I heard him sigh as I bumped into the nightstand.

"Do we think we should ever allow Lottie to choose our costumes again?"

I grabbed for the bedside lamp, catching it in my fins before it hit the floor. "I asked you to choose and you said you didn't care." Man, it was hard to do things with fins instead of hands.

"Well, I do care." I glanced over to see him try to pull the fake white beard over his nipples. That made me snicker. His blue gaze flew to me. "Your dorsal fin is turning me on."

That broke me up. I was about to tell him I'd show him my fin after the party, but our daughter arrived then, Chloe holding her hand. I had never seen a prettier mermaid in my life.

"You look wonderful," I told her.

She flung her long red hair from her face. "I'm Princess Ariel," she informed us then ran over to give Jared, King Triton, a hug. Gordie arrived in his red lobster costume, one of Jared's running shoes in his jaws.

"Everyone looks amazing," Chloe exclaimed while tugging the Nike from Gordie's slobbery mouth. The shoe was a little soggy but in one piece. The doorbell rang. We all hurried down the stairs, tripping over Gordie who always had to hit—and I mean *hit*—the door first.

I got ahold of the dog's blue collar then opened the front door. There on the step stood Dale, who seemed to be taken aback by Flounder greeting him. Then recognition lit up his face.

"Ahh, now I see. These two make sense now." He motioned to Milo in a white seagull costume and Soren who was dressed in a white shirt, red sash around his lean waist, and blue trousers turned up over the calf. He'd *even* found some black boots. He made a damn good Prince Erik. We motioned them inside. Chloe hustled around to get ready for the onslaught of kids about to hit the streets, filling bowls with candy that she would hand out.

A mad scramble to find Ariel's shoes—Lottie was having a bit of a thing about wearing shoes under her tail because mermaids didn't have feet—resulted in us being late. Again. I'd never really understood how people could always be tardy until we had Charlotte. Just when you think you're ready to sail out the door on time, something—usually related to the child— popped up. Missing shoes being one of a thousand time-gobbling things. The little black flats were found stuffed inside her toy box by Chloe. The boys stood in the foyer, Milo with his candy bag, Soren stoically watching the madness. That he'd dressed up was shocking. He'd not been into the whole Halloween *thing* at all until Milo and Lottie had pleaded with him. The boy was a softie with his brother and Charlotte. With us? Not so much yet. But we were giving him time to adjust and trust.

We herded the kids to the SUV, got everyone inside and buckled, and then waved to Dale at the curb. This was our first unsupervised outing. We'd had several supervised ones, from reptile farms to a tour of the Capitol Building to a football game at our local high school. Sadly, we couldn't exactly go door-to-door like most people. The crush of fans that would swarm around me made that kind of thing undoable. What we did instead was go to a team party. This year, as most, it was at Stan's house and yes, Gordie was more than welcome. One more dog wouldn't make a difference.

The kids talked among themselves in the back, Lottie chattering on about how she thought mermaids should carry pokey forks like King Triton.

"She's not going to let that go, is she?" Jared asked.

I shook my head. My fish face slid around to the side. Good thing I wasn't driving.

When we pulled into Stan's long driveway, the boys gasped softly. Yeah, it was a mansion even Elvis would feel at home in. Over the years the enormous house had begun to resemble Graceland a great deal, right down to the Grecian pillars and stone lions in front. There were cars and trucks lined up along the sweeping drive. We parked behind Adler's new SUV. Jared and I looked into the back. Gordie was licking the side window, his lobster antennas limp and soggy. He'd probably been mouthing them. Lottie smiled at us and flipped her feet—excuse me—flipped her tail. The boys appeared kind of leery.

"I know this looks like a lot, but there will be a ton of kids here. You can just hang with them, or you can chill with us and the team. Whatever you feel most comfortable with."

"I'll watch over the kids," Soren announced with a certainty that didn't quite match his wary expression.

"Okay, cool. I'm sure Mama will sit in there. She's not much on big parties."

"'Mama'?" Milo asked.

"You'll see," Jared said with a smile.

So, inside we went, our little pack of seaside characters. The front door was open, and we just walked in. Spooky Halloween songs filled the air. There were cobwebs, jack-o-lanterns, and people in all kinds of costumes. Lottie spied candy at the same time Stan's dog pack sighted Gordie. A mad wag-and-butt-sniff moment took place until Stan—all suited up in a purple mini-dress and massive black wig with his long legs covered by purple fishnet stockings—arrived on the scene. He'd somehow found plum go-go boots to fit his enormous feet. Someone had done pretty well on his makeup, but his beard was now coming in through his foundation and powder.

"Ah here you are with the new boys!" Stan walked up to Milo and Soren, took them by the shoulders, and kissed each boy's cheeks. "Such fine-looking men! I hear much of you. This is my home and my dogs who are putting noses in backsides! Stop doing such rude things in foyer. My husband is here somewhere, making ghost popcorn with caramel dribbles for the children. Would you like to go to the playroom or meet grownups?"

"Uncle Stan! Tell me I am a fine-looking mermaid," Lottie reminded the goalie who swept her up, kissed her cheeks, and fussed over her as he carted her to the playroom.

We followed, waving to the Railers and their partners, as Stan led us to a vast room at the back of the house. Inside were about twenty kids, a dozen or so dogs, and Mama sitting in the corner, in a wooden rocking chair and knitting. She lit up when Stan entered the room, her eyesight was becoming a worry for Stan. Something about macular degeneration that required shots in her eyes. I shuddered at the mere thought of it, but Mama had soldiered through the first round like a trouper. Several moms and dads waved at us as they sat on sofas watching their kids play. I glanced down at Soren and Milo. My fish head slid forward. Gordie was let off the leash to spread his love among all the kids and two old dogs resting by Mama. I'd lost count of how many rescue dogs now called this place home.

"Stupid fish head," I muttered as I removed the head. "Okay, so as you can see there are a ton of things to do in here." That was no lie. The bright yellow and green room was like the inside of a FAO Schwarz. "There are some video games over there." I pointed to the far wall where a few older kids were seated on the floor playing a racing game by the looks of it. Milo chewed on his lip. Stan put Lottie down and she instantly ran over to a pack of little girls with plastic swords and shields. Noah and Margo were deeply engrossed in a fantasy card game at a big wooden table in the corner.

Eva made her way through the rowdy kids to greet us. She was such a young lady now. Beautiful as a flower, smiling, healthy, and very much the apple of her father's eyes. I pitied the young man who knocked on her door for a date. Stan was putting up a valiant fight but her sixteenth birthday was coming up and that was the dating age, according to Mama. Also, the makeup age. According to Stan.

"Hello," Eva said, her accent softer now than it had been a few years ago but still very noticeable. Soren swallowed so loudly I heard it clearly over the din. She shook our hands then looked at Soren who, it seemed, had forgotten he had hands. I nudged him. He started, said something about fish gills, and then turned to exit the playroom. Eva glanced at us.

"He's a little overwhelmed," I told her as I tried not to be rude and bolt off. "Perhaps I should go find him." I jerked a thumb toward our stoic prince then backed out of the playroom, leaving Jared to make the small talk.

It took me a few minutes, but I finally located Soren sitting outside among a horde of scarecrows and hay bales. I made my way over, sat on a frosty hay bale, and placed my fish head on the ground.

"So hey, this is some place, huh?" I asked. He nodded, his cheeks pink. From the cold or from the beauty that was Eva Lyamin I couldn't tell. "Stan is a great guy. He's my best friend."

"Good goalie," he muttered, his sight on his scuffed boots.

"Great goalie, yeah. What position do you play?"

"Forward." He was hunched over, his shoulders down, his hair flopping into his face. I spotted a couple of pimples along his nose. Ugh, the bane of my teen years. Acne. And playing sports did not help at all. All that sweat clogging your pores… "So, everything okay?"

"Yeah, fine. I just wanted to come outside."

"Gotcha. She's really pretty. Eva, that is." He shrugged. Uh-huh. "Even a gay guy like me can appreciate a pretty girl. I bet if you went back in and talked to her, she'd be happy to show you around."

"She's not for me," he replied as an icy wind whirled around the manse, whipping dead leaves across the drive. I shivered inside my fish suit. Soren must have been freezing in his thin dress shirt.

"Are you not into girls?" I asked because it seemed relevant.

"I like girls. Guys too. She's rich and I'm poor. End of."

Oh. Okay. Well, I was making some headway. At least he had been open with me about his sexuality. Huge step in the trust department.

"Yeah, her dads make some big bank, but Eva will not look down on you as a friend because you're not living in a mansion," I explained. He snorted. "She came over from Russia just a few years ago. They were very poor." He glanced at me. "Yeah, super poor farm folk. So, she knows what it's like to come from little into a world where everything is right there for the asking. She could be a good friend if you make the effort. Just saying."

He studied the toes of his boots for a long-ass time. My sexy dorsal fin was probably icy cold and limp now.

"I better go check on Milo," he announced as he rose. I stood as well, and we went back inside, him going upstairs at a slow pace, me watching until he was out of sight. Then I made my way to the bar where Jared stood, a borrowed sweater over his manly chest. He handed me a Sprite with a slice of lemon.

"He okay?" Jared asked as "Monster Mash" blasted through the home sound system.

"Yeah, I think so. We need to talk when we get home." That got me an arched eyebrow. "Nah, it's nothing bad just something I think you should know. My toes are cold. Is my fin still sexy or has it gone soft from the frost?"

I turned around to show him my fin. He chuckled then stepped up behind me, his voice dropping into the low, sensual growl that flipped my switch instantly. "It's just as sexy as it was before. But it *is* chilly to the touch. I think you should let me warm it up when we get home."

I thought that was a damn fine idea.

My husband had incredibly warm and wondrous fingers.

Also, my fin was no longer cold or even on my body. The costume lay over the foot of the bed with Jared's beard, wig, and trident.

I groaned deeply, arching up to try and get more of my cock into his mouth. With my ass on two pillows, I had to use one leg to push upward. The other was resting on his shoulder. He hummed. My balls drew up. I clawed at the bedding, lips pressed shut, eyes closed, as he stroked my prostate over and over and over and over…

"Close…" I coughed out, breathless and shivering with want.

His lips slid from my prick at the same time his thick fingers slipped out of my ass. He moved to cover me, placing my left ankle behind his head as his dick found my hole as if it had a radar. With a flick of his hips, he was buried inside me, his cock stretching me wide.

"Shit… oh shit… so good."

"So damn good," he whispered gruffly, and gripped my ankle tightly.

He didn't have to ask what I wanted or how. He knew. We'd been married long enough now that we could play each other like violins. Edging each other one night then pounding the living hell out of the other the next, orgasm the only goal. Tonight, was one of those come fast nights. He slammed into that sweet spot with such raw power I wondered if a man could faint from too much prostate stimulation. Maybe. If so, what a way to go. I reached for my dick as it slapped my stomach when he thrust. His eyes flared as I thumbed the slit, gathering up pre-cum that I then pushed between his lips. He bit gently on my thumb, his tongue moving over the tip. A groan rumbled up from my chest as he cleaned off my finger. I left my thumb resting between his red lips, taking my cock in my left hand.

"I… so… now," he grunted, flicking his hips hard, driving his dick into me so deep it stole my breath.

My hand fell from his face. I swore I could feel his cock pulsing all the way in my throat. If only…

I blew apart as he filled me with hot spunk. Jerking awkwardly, I felt the warm ropes of cum covering my belly, chest, and chin. Jared made a noise akin to a leopard then fell forward, crushing me as he found, then claimed, my lips in a bruising kiss. Fingers slick with cum, I pushed my hands into his hair, smearing the spend around as his tongue mated with mine.

"Ten," he gasped when the kiss ended, easing out, his cock leaving a fiery trail across the inside of my thigh that I ran my shaky fingers through then brought to my mouth. Sight locked with his, I shoved my fingers between my lips lapping up his cum as he watched. Those blue eyes were hot as liquid sapphire. He tugged me off the pillows, pinning me to the bed with ease. I wasn't fighting him. No fucking way. His mouth slanted over mine. Our tastes mingled. My hands roamed over him, caressing his sides and ass. "Christ."

"Don't bring him into it," I sighed as my body went limp.

"You beautiful man," he whispered, dropped a kiss to my clavicle, and then rolled to his back, his breathing still labored.

"You love me for my dorsal fin," I replied breathlessly. I threw my arm over my chest then made a face when it fell into some sticky cum. "Ugh, I'm a mess."

He sat up slowly. I lay there spent, enjoying the way his muscles bunched and rolled under his skin as he moved. When he stood I smiled at the fine blond hairs on his bubble butt. Nothing was sexier than Jared's ass. Maybe it was the hockey player butt thing —we all had some substantial asses, which meant all our pants had to be custom-made to even fit our backsides and thighs—or maybe it was just that his ass was attached to him.

Jared went into the bath to wash up then brought a warm, wet cloth out to me. I hadn't moved. In fact, I think I had drifted off to sleep for a second. He sat beside me then wiped the cooling seed from my stomach and chest, his touch nearly reverent, as if he were wiping down Michelangelo's *David*.

"You truly are the most beautiful man I have ever seen," he said.

"Again, you just love me for appendages," I replied and got a hearty chuckle from him before he tossed the washcloth into the hamper then stretched out beside me. We'd pull on some shorts before we went to bed in case Lottie came in, given she had issues with locked doors. She disliked them greatly and banged on them loudly during the night if she woke up. Best not to be caught with your balls flapping if the need to sprint out of bed arose.

"Such a sexy fin," he teased as his big body

melted into the bed. I moved into his side, letting my head come to rest on his bicep.

"So, Soren is bi," I threw out conversationally. That brought his head up. His gaze locked with mine. "Yeah, he kind of confessed he liked both sexes to me at the party."

"Um wow, okay. Well, there's that to deal with then," Jared muttered then laid his head back down to his pillow. I ran a finger around his nipple. He twitched a few times before slapping playfully at my hand. "How did that even come up?"

"Well, he'd been so flustered around Eva then bolted so when I found him I kind of asked if he thought she was pretty, and he replied she wasn't for him. So, I prodded just a bit and enquired if he wasn't into girls. To which he said he liked guys and girls."

"That should give him and Ryker something to bond over."

"Yeah, he'll fit right in with all the other rainbow warriors we're related to, play with, or know." Jared made a sleepy sound of agreement. "Do you think we should ask Dale about them possibly moving in? I mean, we've done a ton of supervised and unsupervised visits. Maybe it's time?"

"We'll need to get the contractors moving on their

bedrooms," he replied then shifted to his side to stare at me. "We have to be one hundred percent sure, Tennant. The boys are already close to Lottie, and she to them."

"I know. I want them to live here. I know there will be some issues after the honeymoon period ends. They warned us about that at the adoptive parents' support group we attended on Zoom last weekend. I think we can give them a wonderful home. We're pretty damn cool."

"*You're* pretty damn cool."

"You're cool. I mean, granted, you're not as cool as me because, well, I am Tennant Madsen-Rowe. Have you seen my tattooed neck?" I rolled my head so he could gaze on the Rowe family lion inked into my flesh. A great cover-up of a skate slice that could have done me in if it had nicked my jugular.

"I have seen it. I sucked on it a few minutes ago. Right on his sexy tail."

I drew back slightly. "So, what's sexier? My fin or my tail?"

"Your adoring heart."

My eyes grew a little dewy. I rolled over the top of him and kissed him with all the love I carried for him in that adoring heart of mine.

Chapter Eight

Jared

The paperwork was signed and with our lawyers—the report of intent to adopt was our commitment to having Soren and Milo live with us, and today was the day the boys moved in.

It wasn't going so well.

It was supposed to be easy—Soren and Milo's rooms were done, Lottie was dressed as Ariel because it was a special occasion, and even Gordie was in on the act when Lottie weaved a chiffon scarf around his collar. Lottie had helped to paint *welcome to your new family* sign and fussed over tiny cupcakes Chloe had baked. I didn't know who was more excited, us or Lottie. Or maybe Gordie, who clearly knew *something* was going on and couldn't stop wagging his tail.

A little after ten, as agreed, Dale drove through the gates. Ten and I were waiting with Lottie, and we had Ryker on Zoom ready to welcome his new brothers. All the plans were coming together—we would go from a family of three to five, and I would have four children. Just like everything happening with the Railers right now, from Tanner to the losses, everything seemed to be going wrong.

Soren and Milo clambered out of the car, and then there was a heated discussion, and hugs, and then it was Milo who walked toward us, his face crumpled, and tears coursing down his cheeks. He headed straight for Ten who caught him and held him in a hug. What the hell? I tried to make out Milo's sobbed words but was caught with the fact that Soren was by the car, his arms crossed over his chest, his chin tilted in the familiar defensive thing he had going on.

I left the front door and headed straight for him. "Soren?" I asked with the weight of a hundred questions, and he stiffened.

I caught Dale's gaze across the car. He gave a subtle indication he didn't know what was happening. "Come inside."

He stiffened. "It's for the best."

"What is?"

"I know you and Ten are the good guys," he offered after a pause, "but I'll never be able to call you Dad or whatever rich guy names you come up with."

"Then call us Jared and Ten, we don't expect anything."

"Well, you should," Soren snapped.

"Let's go inside and talk about this."

"No. You have Milo, he's the best kid." Soren held out a piece of paper and it held a list and scribbled numbers. "He hates vegetables, but he loves lasagna, so hide that shit inside it, okay? He has nightmares sometimes, and then if you need me you can call me, and I can talk him down. Make sure he brushes his teeth and looks after himself."

"I don't understand." I glanced over my shoulder, where Ten was still consoling Milo, Lottie was crying. Ten had his phone in his hand, and I wondered if Ryker was still on the line. *I wish he was here. He and Jacob both.* "What's wrong? How about you try to talk to me?" I sat on the small decorative wall surrounding a flower bed by the gate because I'd instinctively felt as if I was looming over Soren, and the last thing he needed was an adult towering over him. His gaze never left me, but he relaxed a little.

"Milo deserves all the good things," Soren murmured. "But I know where you live and if you hurt him…"

Wait, what? "We would never hurt either of you," I said after a pause. Had we done something that meant Soren didn't trust us? That couldn't be right, because he was letting Milo walk up to the porch, and trusting us to… to what? Adopt Milo, but not Soren?

"No, I get that, and you're the best for Milo. Just…" His voice cracked and he cleared his throat, and the pain in his expression was laced with sadness. "Not me, okay. Just, not me."

Dale moved a little closer, but I shot him a glance that I hoped conveyed I'd got this.

Although I very much *hadn't* got this at all.

"We want both of you here, brothers." I kept my tone even, and part of me thought that me saying this might solve whatever was happening.

"Nah." He shrugged, as if he didn't care at all. "I'm okay, I don't need all this fancy shit." He gestured at the house.

I got the feeling he might mean me and Ten as well. Or maybe he was pointing out that he was uncomfortable with our money? We couldn't help that part of our lives, and jeez, it was the house and the money and our loving stable marriage that meant we could even offer Milo and Soren a home at all. I felt guilt and pride at the same time, and it was weird.

"We want you to be our sons," I responded simply.

"You have Milo."

"We want *both* of you to live here."

He sneered, and it was a horrible look for him, but it was an act because the nastiness didn't reach his eyes, which swam with emotion. "We don't always get what we want, so it's best if you keep Milo and when I age out of the system I'll find him again." Soren's words sounded far too rehearsed, as if he'd been practicing them, because he sounded way older than fourteen at that moment.

"Help me understand here," I pleaded, and wondered if I should exercise parental responsibility and simply march him into the safety of his new home.

Yeah force him into the house… that will work. Not.

"Milo said he wants to play hockey, and you can focus on him. Help… him."

"We can do whatever he wants," I reassured him. "But we can do the same for you, so I don't—"

He thrust his arm at me, palm up, and waggled it. "See that scar there?" he asked.

I couldn't actually see anything, so I reached up and held his hand and tugged him closer. He balked, but then he must have thought it was okay, because he took that step so I could see his hand clearly. "What scar?" I asked, peering at his palm, and wishing I had my glasses on. *Vanity 1, practicality 0.*

"There." He pointed and waited for me to acknowledge I'd seen it.

I'd seen a ton of scars in my time, knocks, bruises, broken bones poking through the skin. I've seen blood, and chaos, but for the life of me I couldn't see what he meant. "Yeah," I lied because it seemed important to him.

"I got that when I punched a computer screen, and I cut it so deep my hand was bleeding, but they didn't take me to the hospital, said it was my fault, and it was."

"Okay."

"And this one?" He turned his hand over, but I still couldn't make out anything but his fingers with a teenager's stubby bitten nails. "I got into a fight and got cut."

"A fight?"

"Yeah. With a knife." He added the last bit with venom, as if that would make me hate him. I kept calm, and rational, and wondered how the hell I was going to get to the bottom of this sitting here alone with no Ten, and no Ryker on the phone with me.

"So, I don't understand. Why does this stop you from wanting to come inside with your brother?"

"Because he's perfect and I'm not, okay!" he yelled, and ripped his hand from my hold. The change of mood was impressive, but I'd had Ryker, and I'd seen this before. Temper was what teenage Ryker used when he wasn't getting his way, but also when his grandad interfered with his life, or he didn't want to spend Christmas with me, or something deep had upset him. It was a defense mechanism and one I understood well.

"But why did you punch the screen?"

"That's a stupid fu—question."

I lifted an eyebrow—something I'd learned from being Ryker's dad and dealing with a team like the Railers, particularly Adler. Sometimes a simple raised eyebrow diffused all kind of stupidity and disrespect. Again, particularly from Adler. Stan called it my waggle of doom, Ten called it sexy.

"I don't think it's a stupid question," I defended.

He huffed. "You really want to know how it happened?"

"That's why I asked."

"You *really* want to know?"

He was working his way up to temper again, and I merely nodded, because if I spoke, I might just say the wrong thing.

He huffed. "This guy, foster dad, all bluster and mess, he hit Milo, so I hit him, and then he shoved me, and I told Milo to…" His voice hitched.

"What?" I asked, and he stopped and stared at me. "Soren, what did you tell Milo to do?"

"To get in our room and lock the door. He was only four, okay? He was just this little kid, and I couldn't look after him. But I kicked the guy, okay? I told him to leave my brother alone, and he shoved me into this room, like an office, and he started hitting me and I punched that screen so hard, I was so angry, I was so fucking mad!"

I let the cursing slide—I don't even think Soren realized what he was saying, and my heart broke for the two kids in the system.

"And the other scar?"

"Some psycho mom who said Milo was talking back at her when she was making dinner. He was just excited about this hamster at school who'd eaten carrots from his hand, and she shouted at him and waved the knife she was using at him, and I just grabbed it. I wanted to stab her, I wanted to make all the shouting stop. Why wouldn't she just listen to his stupid hamster story and smile like a real mom would?"

My heart stopped. "You didn't really want to stab her, did you?"

He blinked at me. "I had the knife."

"So, what did you do with it?"

"What?"

"The knife?"

"Didn't you hear what I said? I wanted to stab her."

"What did you do with the knife?" I repeated.

"Nothing. I just held it, and then dropped it, and got Milo to the yard to talk about the stupid hamster and hug him and tell him it was all okay."

"And you were bleeding."

"I put a dishcloth on it, and the mom, well she felt bad, and Milo got extra ice cream."

"Did you tell anyone what'd happened? Did you tell Dale?"

Soren glanced at the social worker and flushed red, then shook his head at me. "No point, what are they going to do? Find us another family? Another place where they'd shout at Milo? Somewhere I have to get between him and the *adults* that are meant to be looking out for us?"

"That won't happen here," I hoped my voice carried all the conviction I felt in my heart.

"I know. And see, that's why you can have Milo, but you can't have me."

"I don't understand?" I paused for a moment. "Why?" Maybe just that single word would be enough to get to the root of all this.

He paced, urgent, nervous movements as he walked from the car to the gate and back, then abruptly he stopped right in front of me. "Because I'm worried and scared all the time for Milo, and angry, and I'll end up destroying everything, and I'm holding Milo back and I really think you're the good guys, and this is *his* time to shine." Tears collected and spilled in his eyes, and he was red in the face and rigid with the pain of everything.

"You're wrong." I offered, not second-guessing what I was going to say and hoping to hell it was the right thing. "Not about us being the good guys, I mean, we have our faults, but we try hard. I mean the bit about Milo being happy. Have you ever wondered why he is such a happy kid? Why he's so open and full of sunshine? That's because you were always there—a barrier between him and the bad things in life. The things you felt you had to do, don't make you a terrible person, they don't make you a terminally angry person. If he had to be apart from you, then what next? Do you think he would smile as much as he does if he thought that his big brother was out there alone? Maybe with another foster family altogether? I mean, he's up there crying in Ten's arms. He's so upset."

Fear and longing filled Soren's expression. "I don't want to mess this up for him," he mumbled and waved at the house again, and then me. "And if you even try to… I know you wouldn't…" He paused. "I don't think you'd hurt him, but… if you did." He seemed confused then, as if he hadn't thought everything through properly. He was telling me he needed to stay away so he didn't mess things up, but that meant leaving his brother alone, and hell, all of that in one teenage head had to be killing him.

I stayed patient and tried finding a solution that worked for him. "You can't look out for him if you're not with him. So, how about a compromise. You're over twelve, which means in six months you get to stand up in front of the judge and tell them if you want to be legally adopted by Ten and me. Stay with us for those six months, watch your brother, see how it works, see if you're happy with how it's going, and then in one hundred and eighty-three days you can make your decision, and we'll cross that bridge when we come to it."

"But you'll adopt Milo whatever? Even if I get angry and... you'll keep him safe? I have to know he's safe."

"You have my word." I held out my hand to shake, and after a moment's hesitation Soren took it and we shook. His world must be such a mess, losing the mother he was old enough to remember, no one being with him, no one to take him and Milo. Today that changed—today Ten and I would make the boys part of our family. "Now, we should go in, because Lottie made cupcakes."

He frowned. "Made them?" He was probably recalling the last trip out with the picnic where Lottie served up homemade caterpillars made of olives and cheese, covered in syrup.

"God no." I shuddered, and he sent me a half smile at our shared horror. "Chloe made them, Lottie decorated them. There's twenty-three of them, your age and Milo's combined. That was a joint decision by Chloe and Lottie."

Gordie trotted over, the scarf trailing behind him, and bumped Soren's leg, looking for attention. Soren scratched the pup's head and was lost in thought. "I can't promise to always be—I dunno—calm and not angry. I know this is a good place, but I have all of this inside…"

I hurried to reassure him. "You have every right to be angry with life, Soren, and now you and Milo have a forever home if you want it. All you have to do is take that first step over to your brother, and Ten and Lottie. The rest we can work on as a family."

"'A family'."

"Yep."

And when he took that first step toward the house, then almost ran to hug Milo, then Lottie, with Gordie in the mix, I caught Ten's confused gaze.

"It's all good," I mouthed, and he nodded. We'd make this work, and in six months I hoped we'd done enough so Soren would say he wanted to stay.

Chapter Nine

Ten

"Remind me again why I thought having the whole Wu-Tang Clan come here for Thanksgiving was a good idea," I moaned as we—we being all the men in the house plus a Lab who'd pounced on a dropped can of cranberry sauce—lugged in groceries.

"What a boo-bang clang, Daddy?" Lottie asked while climbing like a spider monkey onto one stool at our kitchen island. Soren slipped around her silently, ever watchful, and got her seated and strapped into her booster seat.

"I've failed as a parent," I lamented to Jared.

He placed the monstrously large turkey on the counter, exhaled dramatically, and then turned to face me. "I was going to ask who that was too," he confessed. My flat look made him snicker.

"They're an old 90s hip hop group," Soren explained as he buckled Lottie into her seat. The kid was big into hip hop and rap music, we'd learned.

"Wait. Just… wait." I placed my bag of food onto the counter then folded my arms over my chest. "Since when is 90s music old?"

"Since like forever ago," Soren tossed out before strutting out to grab more bags of food. Milo was playing tug-o-war with Gordie. "No one listens to that old crap anymore."

I gaped at Soren's lean back as he walked off. Jared was having a good laugh across the room.

"Dude. That sliced deep," I mumbled then barked out a command to Alexa to play some Smash Mouth. Stat.

Reveling in the music of my apparent dotage, we put away groceries while "All Star" and "Walking on the Sun" rolled through the entire house. These whippersnappers would learn about good music if I had to play Nirvana and Marianas Trench twenty-four seven. Old crap. Pfft.

Dinner was some grilled chicken breasts, green beans, and tater tots. The tots were for the princess. Every meal should have tater tots or dino fries, according to our daughter. The boys weren't super picky. They seemed grateful to have lots of food, especially Soren, who had shot up at least two inches in the past month. Not that they'd hadn't been fed at their foster homes, because they had, but being able to go back for seconds or thirds seemed new, which I got. Feeding kids was expensive. Our grocery bill had tripled since the boys had moved in. Which wasn't an issue for us but for a lot of folks it would be. The stipend foster parents got per child was pretty miserly considering the cost of food and clothing, and we saved it all in an account for them, although they didn't know that. And then there was sports. Sports were expensive as hell, as well we both knew.

Soren had reluctantly agreed to join the hockey team at the Chesterford Academy, the private school he and Milo had started at. He still had trouble accepting gifts from us. Maybe that was because he still felt as if he wasn't good enough. Which was *so* not the case. He was an amazing kid with a clever mind and above average skills on the ice. I was hoping to take them to the Railers training facility over this short Thanksgiving break to spend some time with them. Our travel schedule was brutal. Jared and I both longed to spend time with the kids but that wasn't to be, sadly. Any free time was a blessing, and we made sure we did what we could to bond with them all.

That night we'd made it a family night at home. The Rowe clan would descend upon us tomorrow, as would Ryker and Jacob, who also had a small window to fly out, visit, and then fly back, as the Raptors were playing on Saturday as the Railers were. The kids staked out one of the two new sofas we'd bought for the rec room, Gordie clambered up to join them, our rules about dogs on the furniture disappearing fast.

Jared and I shared the plush blue couch, his arm resting on my shoulder. He looked sexy as all fuck with his glasses on. I kissed him on the cheek just because. Milo and Soren seemed intrigued by our relationship. We were openly affectionate with each other, perhaps more so than some other couples. Since we had to be exceptionally discreet in public we touched more at home. Nothing over-the-top of course, but we held hands, hugged, cuddled, and kissed often. Lottie was used to it, but the boys always watched with open curiosity. Jared and I hoped that by seeing us being so tactile they'd grow up to expect the same from their future partners.

The early evening movie was *The Little Mermaid* because Lottie was still on that kick. Jared dozed during the viewing, waking up in time to get Lottie tucked in while I queued up *Spider-Man: Into the Spider-Verse* for the older kid time. Milo was big into superheroes and I kind of loved Miles Morales as the friendly neighborhood web-slinger. We were all about representation in this house. After Lottie was down for the night, Jared returned, and we all snacked on popcorn, sipped Dr. Pepper, and cheered on the good guys.

The boys were too old for us to fuss over before bed, which kind of sucked because one of my favorite things ever was reading to Lottie at bedtime. But we understood and gave them a warm goodnight before they shuffled to their rooms. Soren usually took care of his brother, tucking him in then hanging out with him, reading comics until Milo drifted off. Soren might put on that angry face to the world but for little kids he was a pile of goopy softness.

Gordie had taken to sleeping at the top of the stairs. Jared called it "defending the sleeping hoomans against intruders" and I couldn't disagree. Amazing that a three-month old dog could be so protective of his pack mates. Either that or he wanted to get down the stairs first thing for breakfast. It was a toss-up probably, but defender of the hoomans sounded nobler.

Worn out from a few rough games during the

week and the shopping splurge this morning, Jared and I collapsed into bed. I kissed him goodnight, admired his profile as he read for a bit, and then rolled over. I was out instantly. I came awake during the night, the heater running nearly masking the sound of Gordie whimpering in the hallway. Sitting up, I rubbed at my eyes sleepily, and slid from the bed as silently as possible. The clock beside the bed read *2:38* in bright red numerals. Jared snored softly. The cold November moon was bright in the night sky, filling the room with soft white light. I padded to the door, opened it, and stumbled into the hallway. Gordie sat outside Milo's door, whining, his paw on the door as if he were trying to push it open. Once I was in the hall then I could hear a child crying.

"Good boy," I whispered to the pup, giving his head a pat before cracking open Milo's door. Gordie wiggled around me, pushing into the room. Milo was in bed, the moon illuminating his slight form under the thick duvet he so loved to sleep under. "Stay," I told the dog. He leapt onto the bed. Right. We needed to work on *stay*. Milo whimpered as the dog nuzzled under the covers. I flipped on the nightlight that Milo insisted he did not need then moved to the bed, pulling the dog back by his collar, and pushed his backside down to a sit.

"Now stay," I told Gordie with alpha firmness before turning my attention to Milo. His cheeks were wet, his eyes open, his lips trembling. "Hey little man, did the dog scare you?"

"N-n-no," he stammered, tears rolling down cheeks damp from dog spit. "I had a bad dream."

Milo launched himself at me, his thin arms linking around my neck, his face buried in my shoulder. Poor kid. I gathered him and his duvet up, wiggled around the best I could, and then rested my back against the wooden headboard. He curled into me, sniffling, his skinny legs drawn up tight. Gordie settled beside us, whining gently, the whiskers over his eyes twitching. I yanked the duvet about us, cocooning us, and held Milo until his tremors subsided.

"Was it a monster bad dream?" I asked and got a head shake. "Was it a bad dream about a super villain?" I'd been sure the movie we'd watched had been pretty tame, nothing too scary for a kid his age. He shook his head again. "Was it a bad dream about something real?"

"Maybe," he replied so quietly I had to strain to hear him. I tucked the duvet up under his chin and held him closer. "Mean Mike was hitting Soren again."

Shit. I had a vague knowledge of Mean Mike—

the abusive bastard who had hurt Soren and Milo in a previous foster home. Jared had relayed the tragic story to me after Soren had told him on moving-in day. It incensed me that anyone could hit children as sweet as these two boys were. Hell, we didn't even use a rolled-up newspaper on the dog as some people had told us to do.

Violence was never the answer, said the hockey player.

Tossing down the gloves on the ice was a rarity for me but yeah, I fought occasionally. Was it right? Probably not. Should it be part of the game? I didn't know. Lots of us went back and forth on the subject. There was less and less fisticuffs on the ice for sure. Would it ever go away completely? The fans would be the ones to decide.

But getting into a scrum with a man the same size as you were, was one thing, lashing out at a kid was another.

"I'm sorry you had that happen to you," I replied, stroking his back. "Adults should never do that."

"Soren says that you and Jared are good guys. Mean Mike was a shitter," Milo stated with a bit more attitude than he'd had a minute ago.

I smiled then wiped the smile away before he saw it. "That's not a nice word. Your grandma would faint if she heard you cussing. She used to give us extra chores for using bad words," I told him as we sat there in the glow of a Captain America nightlight.

"She's coming tomorrow with our new grandpa, right?"

"Yep, and bringing pies," I said then made yummy sounds that pulled a giggle from him. "Grandma makes *the* best pies, and cakes, and cookies. And she's really nice. So is my dad. And all my brothers. Brady is the oldest one and he can be a turd."

"Big brothers are turds," he mumbled then used my old tee to wipe his nose as he hid under the duvet.

"Yours is pretty okay," I reminded him. On the whole they got along well, but we'd seen some sibling stuff popping up the more comfortable they got here. "I have two older brothers. They're nice. And they have wives and daughters. So many daughters. There will be girls all over the place tomorrow. You okay with all those girls?"

"My cousins?" He peeked out at me, his lashes still clumpy and damp.

"Yep, cousins. And a stepbrother too, and his husband who will be your step-something. No, maybe he's not a step anything. Well, Jacob is awesome. He runs a ranch out in Arizona with Ryker.

So, he's like a real cowboy with horses and everything."

"Cool. Can we go ride horses at Ryker and Jacob's ranch?"

"You bet. We'll head there first thing once the season is over."

He smiled at me. "Can I have seconds on pie?"

I dropped a kiss to his dark hair. "You can have seconds on whatever you want, Sport."

"Jamie, if you reach for that pie once more I will slap your fingers," Mom barked at my brother at the end of the very long table we were all seated at.

"It's for Milo," Jamie explained then lifted a fat slice from the second pumpkin pie to grace the table.

Mom looked at Milo. "Is it for you, honey?"

He nodded, bright-eyed, his cheeks pink from an hour outside running with the girls to work off some of their energy. Poor Milo was the only male in a gaggle of seven girls, eight if you counted Lottie. Brady had four, Jamie was up to three now, one just barely walking.

"Okay, if it's for my grandbabies then it's fine," Mom said, stirring her tea as she gave her middle son the I'm-watching-you expression we all knew so well.

Soren sat between Jared and me, his gaze moving around the table constantly as if he were trying to catalog each member of his new family. We hoped we would be his new family anyway. He could still back out if he wished. He was over twelve and knew his own mind. We prayed he would stay. The obvious madness of a Madsen-Rowe holiday hopefully wouldn't terrify the kid into packing up and hopping the first bus out of town.

"Jean, does the seconds on pie extend to grandbabies on the other side of the family tree?" Ryker asked sweetly, gazing at my mother through a mop of curls as if she hung the moon.

"Of course. You and Jacob can have seconds. Brady, Jamie, and Tennant—you can fight over the crumbs."

"How is *that* fair?" Brady asked while Ryker, grinning maniacally, hoisted two fat slabs of apple pie to a plate he was sharing with Jacob.

"It's the grandmother rule. Grandbabies come first." Mom stated, gave me a wink, and then sipped her tea calmly.

Dad pulled on the waistband of his jeans. "I knew I should have worn the stretchy pants," he moaned then unbuttoned his button with a sigh.

Gordie was doing his best impersonation of a

Hoover under the table. The two Lisas were telling a story about something they'd seen on Instagram that had to do with flowers and tractor tires. I sat back, stuffed to the gills, and just listened. The house was warm, overly warm because of the people, and the oven being on for hours, and loud. Kids chattering, dog snuffling, adults laughing. It was perfect. The most perfect Thanksgiving we'd ever hosted in our home.

Clean-up would be monumental. The kitchen was a fright. Pans and pots, roasting pans, a turkey carcass to pick clean so we could feast on hot turkey sandwiches tomorrow. Loads of work, but we'd get through it together.

I glanced at my eldest brother when he rose. "I need to stand up and let all of that food settle." He patted his slightly rounded belly then ambled into the living room after giving me a look and a subtle jerk of his head.

"Yeah, me too." I stood, placed my napkin on the table, and followed Brady into the living room then outside. It was cold, the air fogging in front of us as we closed the door. I shoved my hands into the front pockets of my jeans.

"Shit, it's gotten colder. Winter is coming," Brady commented as he drank in our front yard. There wasn't much to see. All the leaves had fallen, the flowers were gone, and the holiday decorations were still in the garage. November was a transition month in my mind.

"So say them upon the wall," I tossed out as my arms bristled with gooseflesh. Brady chuckled softly, his breath lingering before a bitter cold wind swept it away. "Did you want something in particular or did you want to lure me out here to freeze to death? This way your team won't have to face me in a month?"

"My team can handle you," he stated. That was his opinion. Given how we'd been playing it might be true, but I was hoping we'd shake off the funk and get our heads out of our asses. "I wanted to ask you something. Lisa and I have been talking and we'd like to have you and Jared listed as the girls' guardians if something were to happen to us."

My jaw dropped. "Oh, that's… wow. Why are we talking about this now?"

He blew out a breath that billowed his cheeks. "Because it's something that all parents need to consider. I travel a lot. Lisa does now too with her new job. Her parents are too old to handle four girls, and Mom and Dad aren't getting any younger. You've turned into a solid man, trustworthy, smart, and devoted to your husband and children. You have a good head on your shoulders, you're financially stable, and the girls love you."

I stuck my finger in my ear and wiggled it. "Holy shit, did you just say I have a good head on my shoulders? Did I hear that right? Must be my ear hairs are frozen."

He rolled his eyes. "Maybe I was mistaken."

"Seriously, is this the same dude who told me I was making a mistake signing with a team that wasn't an original six team?"

He glanced at the gray sky. Snow was in the forecast. "I stand by that statement."

I had to laugh. "Rock head," I muttered then gave him a long, serious look. "I'll discuss it with Jared tonight when the kids are all down, but I don't foresee him being against it. He likes you. I'm not sure why…"

He chuckled. Then he offered me his incredibly icy hand. I slapped mine over it. "Thank you, Ten. That's a worry off my shoulders."

"My pleasure. Now, can we drop this depressing topic? What even made you think about such shit?" Not that it wasn't something that Jared and I would need to do as well. Our wills would need to be changed to include the boys as soon as the legalities were completed.

"Moral Dunkirk," he replied, his voice suddenly sad. "One minute he's full of life and living la vida loca, and the next he's being cut out of plane wreckage. That scared the shit out of me, Ten. Me and a lot of the other guys on the team."

Yeah. I could see that. It had rocked all of us in the hockey world who had known and/or played with or against Dunny. "Lisa and I had a moment of reckoning and realized that we weren't immortal and that we needed to ensure our kids were in the best hands possible. Seeing how amazing you are with Lottie and now those two boys, well, we knew you were our first choices. But don't do it if you don't want to. Jamie would take them as well, but Lisa's mom isn't doing too great after that last round of chemo and... well, it would be a lot if they have to take her mother into their house."

"Yeah, hey, no, I totally get it. And I get why Dunny's accident shook everyone up. It did me too. He's doing good now though, right?"

Brady smiled. "Yeah, he's doing really well. Got himself a boyfriend, a new career coaching our Rebels sled team, and he's about to become an uncle."

"Good, I'm glad."

The door behind us opened. Soren peeked out at us with curious dark eyes. "The lady—your mom—I mean, Grandma…" He seemed to struggle over the word, but at least he used it this time. While Milo was relaxed, Soren still kept one eye on the door, and it made me sad sometimes. I smiled in encouragement, and he cleared his throat. "Anyway, she said to check on you two because the last time you two snuck off you both ended up wedged into a trash can on top of the roof."

"That was totally Brady's idea," I quickly said then looped an arm around Soren. "He wanted to see if two of us could speed off the roof and land safely in the pool."

"I'd been watching this show about daredevils and Niagara Falls, and Jamie was too fat to fit into the can with me," Brady explained as we made our way back inside.

"Hey, I heard that! I was never fat. That was muscle!" Jamie called from the dining room then appeared in the doorway with a slab of stuffing on his plate. "Also, I was too smart to let you talk me into doing something so stupid."

"Yeah, Ten was pretty gullible," Brady snickered. "Soren, did he ever tell you about the time that Jamie and I had him convinced that a mutated duck lived in the bathtub drain?"

"Okay, I don't think we need to be spreading that story around," I protested.

"I'd like to hear it," Jared called from the dining room. The bastard. I'd not told anyone about the drain duck for a reason.

"Well, Ten was about five, a total sucker, and had this phobia of ducks," Brady began, pushing me out of the way so he could drop an arm around Soren's lean shoulders.

Soren looked startled at first, then he glanced my way and I saw his lips twitching with humor, and let his soon-to-be uncle lead him back into the dining room. I sighed as the story began. Milo was lucky. He had a brother who would never tell him a duck that ate little boys' willies lived in the tub. I'd not bathed for months. Mom was not amused. Dad had to snake the tub every night for a year before I would concede to use it.

Yeah, brothers were a real hoot.

Family. What could you do with them but love them?

Chapter Ten

Jared

A brief run of home game wins from Thanksgiving to near Christmas had us feeling a little more positive, but each of those wins had been scrappy, and had cost us more than I wanted to contemplate. Stan took a nasty hit after a Carolina D-man ended up flying right into our goalie, taking him out—Stan was out over Christmas and into the new year, and he was incandescent with rage. Then, last night, playing a feisty New York team, our captain was another casualty, and given the hundred-mile-an-hour puck that had hit Connor up and under his helmet, he could be out for a lot longer than a few games. His eye socket was shattered—fuck—I'd seen the X-rays, and if we got him back before February, we'd be lucky. It might be more like April, which meant he had a season-ending injury. Would he make it back before the Stanley Cup race? He might, but there might not be a race if we didn't hook up more wins than losses.

"Fourteen. Seven. Seven," Coach Benning repeated. We were all packed into the video review room—players, coaches, management—and the urgently arranged meeting was a sober affair. "Fourteen. Seven. Seven." He stared at us all. "In twenty-eight games we've won half. I wish I could say we won them cleanly but we're fighting too hard all the damn time, and sometimes it seems we're fighting ourselves. Where is Railers hockey? Where are the slick moves and the concentrated passes? Where is the defense? What do we have to do here to get cohesion?"

No one said anything out loud, but above the murmurings Stan, sitting a few rows ahead of me, muttered something in Russian and shifted in his chair, adding a curse when his walking boot knocked the chair. "Bigly fucked," he lamented a little louder.

No one laughed, or agreed, or said one thing about his summing up of the season. He was right. We were fucked.

"The last time the Railers had only a fifty percent

win rate was our first goddamn rookie year." Unspoken was the *before Ten arrived*, or maybe that was just me who considered the existence of the team in two phases, before Ten, and after Ten. That first year for the Railers had been pretty dismal, but Stan had been with the team from day one, as had Connor, Adler, hell, half of the room were guys drawn from all over to form the newest expansion team. Well, newest until Vegas and Seattle, that was. I knew I was biased, but all of them, and the ones who came after, had made the best damn team in the NHL.

The best damn team who couldn't get their shit together.

Ten and Westy, our alternate captains, sat down at the front—with Connor gone for now, the burden of leadership would fall completely on their shoulders. They were already leaders in the locker room, good examples of how the Railers should be as a team… at least Ten was. Westy had been playing the best defensive hockey of his life recently, obsessed, and focused, with tunnel vision. Knowing what Ten said about him and the cancer-stricken Levi having sparks, I wasn't the only one who believed that Westy was cutting everything from his life to think of nothing but hockey. Maybe that was a good thing on paper, but last night's game had proven otherwise. Westy had spent so much time covering Tanner's mistakes he'd run himself ragged. Buffalo could see the vulnerability in our defense and boy did they use it. On his good days Tanner was unstoppable, the man was a beast, tall and dominant and visible on the ice, but on his bad days like last night, he was a mess, too many turnovers, not protecting our forwards, missing passes. Thankfully, there was more good than bad, even so, at this level of hockey we couldn't have a D-man who wasn't present, and the coaching team knew that.

I knew that, and the defense were my responsibility, and it was me they were looking to for a solution. I hated I was considering bringing up Arlo from the feeder team on a semi-permanent basis, not that Arlo wasn't an outstanding player because he was, but what did me doing that mean for Tanner? And how could I break up Westy and Tanner as partners when they'd been such a force to contend with in the past?

Railers' fans were aware of Tanner's brother's illness—the press release had hit social media a week after Tanner found out, and the most loyal of them were still in Tanner's corner, forgiving his mistakes. But the vocal dissenters were becoming louder, and the pressure on Tanner, and as a result Westy his Dpartner, was intense. Last night, with New York in the barn, I'd seen Tanner crumble and Westy try to step up, watched Connor take a puck to the eye, watched as Bryan in goal was exposed to so many shots he had no hope of stopping them. A six-one loss, the worst this season, and we had to stop and take a moment to re-evaluate.

Things had to change. I didn't want to have to be the one to decide, but the stats spoke for themselves.

So, getting home post-meeting where nothing had been decided, to find a crying Milo waiting for us, was like the icing on the freaking cake. We couldn't afford to bring our worries back home off the ice, but was I missing something by trying to balance the kids and work? Were we distracted? Should I be harder on Tanner? Should I push him to one side and focus on bringing up Arlo? Or should I say fuck hockey, and deal with a crying Milo plus a missing Soren as my priority? I hated that this was an issue. I had responsibilities to the team, but it was a game.

Milo and Soren, Ryker, Lottie, Ten—they were my life.

"Hey, bud, what's up?" Ten asked, as Milo flew into his arms and Ten lifted him high and cradled him and hugged him like he would never let him go.

There was no sign of Lottie, or Chloe, and not the

slightest whisper of Soren being here. Ten and I exchanged glances. I nodded I would find everyone, and he would comfort a sobbing Milo who could only say one thing. *I'm don't want him to go. Please don't make him go.*

This didn't sound good, and things went from bad to worse when I found Chloe and Lottie in the playroom reading—or at least Chloe was reading, Lottie was curled on her lap fast asleep.

"Okay?"

"Drama at school with Milo and Soren," she whispered. "He's in his room, but Jared..." She bit her lip and smoothed a hand over Lottie's curls, "The academy called the home number when they couldn't get hold of you."

I pulled out my cell, five missed calls. "We were in a meeting, I'm sorry."

She shrugged. "Part of the job," she said with a soft smile. "They're asking for you and Ten to go in."

Fuck, that didn't sound good.

I backed out of the room and headed upstairs, casting a look into the front room where Ten was on the sofa, hugging Milo, whispering, and with Gordie curled up next to him. He had that under control, and I had to find Soren. I knocked on his door.

"Go away!" Soren called from inside. We had a

no locked doors policy with the kids, and I knocked one more time and interrupted his yelled GO AWAY! by pushing open the door and stepping inside.

He froze, staring at me, his arms full of clothes and his duffle on his bed.

I closed the door behind me, and he shrunk back, and instinctively I knew that I'd fucked up, and I re-opened the door then took a seat at his desk strewn with notebooks from math to chemistry. Soren glanced from me to the door and then back again.

"What's up?" I asked as if I didn't have a care in the world, even if inside my heart hurt from the pain in Soren's expression.

He snapped out of his frozen fear and stuffed the clothes haphazardly into the bag. "I told you," he said evenly. "I told you that this wouldn't work."

I scooted the chair closer and tugged out the shirts he'd put into his bag.

He stuffed them back in.

I pulled them out.

"It's my stuff! okay!?" he yelled. "I'm not taking any of your precious rich dude stuff." He picked up a Railers' jersey, one with Adler's number on the back, and threw it to the floor. Adler was his favorite Railer, or so he told us, and he wore that jersey all the time at home. "I won't take anything that I didn't come with."

I leaned over and picked up the jersey, smoothed it then folded it neatly. "This is yours."

"Yeah, well, I don't want it."

"Adler gave it to you."

"I don't want it."

He stuffed his clothes back in and I pulled them out again, a tug of war ensuing over one of the worn T-shirts he'd arrived with. I could give in, but it seemed vital that I didn't, and we tugged so hard that it ripped.

Shit.

He stared down at the ripped shirt, horrified, and then his eyes changed in an instant and he flew at me, his fists pounding my chest, my arms, anywhere he could get me. I stumbled back before channeling my latent D-man skills and managing to catch his fists and then hold him tight, so he couldn't punch me. He struggled and vibrated with temper, but I felt as if I had to hold onto him.

That maybe he *needed* me to hang on.

After a while he stopped fighting, and cautiously I released my hold. He stumbled away from me until the back of his knees hit the bed and he sat down with a curse. I didn't call him on the curse, in fact I did nothing. I recalled the days when Ryker would be all piss and vinegar, and often it was me giving him space to talk that meant he opened up the best.

Thankfully, Soren filled the void. "I won't make a fuss or anything after I'm gone," he murmured, then picked up the fallen Adler shirt and traced the numbers on the back. "Thank you for what you've done, with Milo I mean."

He was talking as if he wanted to leave, and with the packed bag—well the unpacked bag now—I imagined he'd worked his way through something terrible and could only see one way out.

"What happened?"

He glanced at me. He wasn't crying, but his thin frame was rock-solid with tension, and his shoulders were up around his ears. I'd seen the same posture in so many skaters—it wasn't temper that was driving him now, it was trying to control the temper that held him steady.

"You know what happened," he said.

I shook my head and retrieved my cell from my pocket, waggling it theatrically./ "We've been in a phones-off meeting, and then we just wanted to get home to you guys."

He rolled his eyes. "You should listen to what they say, then you can just leave me alone."

"How about *you* tell me?" I settled more comfortably into the tight-fitting desk chair—not built for adult hockey players—and crossed my legs at the heels, playing the I'm-staying-right-here card. His eyes widened, and he glanced at the door, probably gauging if he could make it in time. I scooted the chair farther from the doorway and right into the corner on the opposite side of the bed then resumed my lounging, and saw his shoulders relax a little. The kid was terrified, and I was fucking angry that people had hurt him before and made him feel like every person in his young life was out to get him.

"I hit this Felix kid at recess, and I don't care what you say, I'm not sorry," he admitted clearly. There was no mumbling, it was as if he was daring me to lose my shit at his defiance.

"Why?"

"He had it coming," Soren said, and took a moment to pull the Adler jersey to his chest. Only when he was holding it did he relax a little—who knew Adler would be a good influence on anyone?

"Okay, and?"

He peered at me suspiciously. "And what?"

"Why did he have it coming?"

"He wouldn't stop, so I hit him."

"Wouldn't stop what?"

"TalkingshitaboutyouandTenbeinggayandshitathockeyandtakinginstrays." The words exploded from him in one run-on sentence, and it took me a moment to understand.

"Talking shit about us being gay, and together, and adopting you and Milo?" I summarized.

"Yeah. Every single day, every time he sees me, and then he…"

"What?"

"Said that you were messing… with me and Milo… and depraved… and I didn't even know what that word really meant, and I had to look it up and when I saw what he meant I hit him." He pointed to a spot at the end of his nose. "There was a lot of blood, it went *everywhere*, but he deserved it."

Horror consumed me, not at the casual acceptance by Soren of violence, but the manner in which it had been provoked. What kind of world was it that kids wanted to hurt another kid so badly. Fuck. I had to fight damn hard not to clap Soren on the back and congratulate him for putting a bully down, but I couldn't do that. I had to be the adult here. I thumbed to a contact on my list, hovering over Stan's name because he *knew people* and then found the number for the school, dialing it, and connecting the right person—a Mr. Michaels—almost immediately.

I didn't explain away Soren's behavior, I didn't rise to the deputy principal's buzzword-laden and passive-aggressive concerns nor his suggestion that Soren take a few days to calm down, ostensibly suspending him. Nope, I laid my opinion on the line, clearly, succinctly, and loudly, so Soren could hear it all.

"There won't be any kind of faked time out, Mr. Michaels. Nor a suspension of any kind. Instead, I want a meeting," I said. "You'll get Felix to be there, plus his parents, and I will attend *with my husband,* and we will hash this out, and again, this is not about suspension, but educating Soren and Felix plus Felix's parents, and the entire school, over what is appropriate."

"Now, Mr. Madsen-Rowe, that isn't—"

"Eight-fifteen tomorrow morning would be good," I interrupted him.

There was some rustling, some murmuring, and finally the meeting was set without fanfare.

As soon as I was off the phone, I needed to deal with Soren, in a way that trod the fine line between actual and prospective parent. I tugged the pile of his clothes toward me, and then put every single item away, each carefully folded. God knows if I got everything in the right place, but Soren watched me and with each tidied shirt the tension in him seemed to ease.

"It was the wrong thing to do, sir," Soren murmured after a while. "I know I shouldn't have hit him."

"You shouldn't have," I agreed, "but how we deal with the passion in us, and what decisions we make in the future, makes us the people we are. So, we'll work on that, as a family. Okay?"

"Yes, sir. I'm sorry for hitting you."

"You'll make a good defenseman," I half-joked because I didn't want to make too much of what he'd done right as I was de-escalating.

"Nah, I want to be all quick and up front like Adler," he said.

"Hey, guys," Ten said from the door, and both Soren and I spun to face them. Milo was holding Ten's hand, and for the first time in a long time he didn't immediately go to Soren.

"I don't want you to go." Milo narrowed his eyes at his big brother.

Soren glanced from me to Ten and then to his little brother and teared up. "I don't want to go either."

There was a charged moment where no one said anything, but it was Ten who broke the silence.

"Pizza," he announced. "But first, a hug."

We'd heard about this in our Zoom group—the family hug—something we did instinctively anyway —Milo and Soren weren't used to it, and we hadn't fully road-tested the idea in situations this tense. Milo let go of Ten's hand and tugged Soren close and then Ten, and finally I joined in. We hugged it out, and I hoped that somehow we'd reassured Soren that we would always have his back, but we'd be there for when he messed up, and we'd be angry or concerned, but there would always be love.

At least, that was what I'd been going for.

The meeting was brief, Mr. Michaels tense with worry. Felix was a short, skinny, blond kid, who leaned back in his chair as if he didn't have a care in the world. I didn't like to tell him that his vulnerability was showing in his faked pose. He glanced at Ten and me once, and for the rest of the meeting he ignored us. His parents never showed. He explained they were on a business trip, and I didn't see a lie, but I detected something like defiance and sadness all rolled into one.

He was made to apologize, which he did with

reluctance, and then it was Soren's turn, and I held my breath.

"Sorry," was all he said at first. "I hit you because you piss—upset me."

"Whatever," Felix muttered under his breath, causing Mr. Michaels' anxious desk-tapping to increase.

"Yeah, whatever," Soren said tiredly. "Ten and Jared are cool, and you can't touch that."

I took that as a win.

Hell, at least I was part of *one* team that was winning at *something*.

Chapter Eleven

"Daddy, reindeers doesn't like carrots."

I glanced up from the artfully arranged carrot platter to my daughter kneeling in her booster seat at the kitchen island.

"Sure, they do," I replied. I honestly had no clue if reindeer liked carrots, but Mom always had carrots on one plate for the flying reindeer, as well as cookies and milk on another plate for Santa, and I would *not* mess with tradition. "It's *you* who doesn't like carrots." I pointed at the pint-sized princess with a long, fat carrot. She wrinkled her nose. "Also, please sit down before you fall and crack your skull." Great, I was now sounding like my mother. I had always suspected it would be me turning into Mom while Brady and Jamie became Dad.

"Speaking from experience, cracking your skull hurts really badly."

Her eyes went round but she sat down. "Did you hurt your skull, Daddy?"

"A long time ago," I told her as worry was now sitting on her face. No child of mine was going to be sad on Christmas Eve. Not if I could help it. "So, what do you think reindeer eat?" I asked just as Soren and Milo came thundering into the kitchen. Two hours had passed since dinner, so this was probably snack run number one of the night.

"Reindeer eat fern, grasses, and shrubs. Also, trees. We're learning about Arctic animals in science class," Milo offered, elbowing his big brother aside to steal a cookie from Santa's dish.

"No! No! Stop eating Santa's cookies!" Lottie shrieked at Milo. "He will see you being bad and not bring me my magic castle play set!"

Milo shoved the whole cookie into his face. Lottie had a small meltdown. I left the boys with the platters to carry the exhausted little girl who was up way past her bedtime to bed. Jared was showering, working to get some pine sap out of his hair after a rather lengthy tussle with the live tree we'd bought and set up two hours ago. We were kind of running late with the decorating. Travel sucked. It really did.

It took some doing but Lottie finally gave up after only two read throughs of *Harold and the Purple Crayon* by Crockett Johnson. I'd loved this book as a child and now here I sat reading it to my own precious one. After I kissed her goodnight then turned on the baby monitor, I made my way to the master bath to see how Jared was coming.

Not well. I found him wearing nothing but a towel —always a pleasant sight—leaning over the sink about to cut a chunk of his hair off.

"Whoa, hold up there Edward Scissorhands," I said as I entered the steamy bathroom. "Did you google how to get pine sap out of your hair?" He gave me that look over the top of his glasses. Sexy bastard. I typed in a search and lo and behold, there was an answer. "Says here to use rubbing alcohol."

He sighed then laid down the shears. "Cutting it out seemed the most direct route."

"Once a D-man always a D-man. No finesse whatsoever." I padded over, rummaged around in the medicine cabinet, and then pulled out a bottle of rubbing alcohol. After finding a cotton ball I stepped in front of him, his gaze following me closely, and began dabbing the sticky glob of sap. I tried my best to keep my attention on his gold-and-silver hair, but my sight kept darting down to touch on his. "You're looking at me just like Milo eyed the cookies for Santa."

"I have an adult present for you after all the kids are in bed," he whispered huskily, moving his hips just enough to press his hard cock into my hip. That woke my dick up.

"You mean after the kids are in bed and after we tote all the presents downstairs from the attic and after we put together a magic castle and a new bike."

The lusty look on his handsome face fell away. "Yeah, after all that."

"I'll get right on that gift of yours and then I'll give you one of mine." I rubbed my hipbone against his erection. He grunted softly, his hands rising to settle on my hips. My gaze moved to his mouth.

"Ten! Do we have any more of those jelly cookies? Milo ate all the ones on the plate!" Soren shouted up the stairwell.

"You ate some too!" Milo bellowed at the top of his lungs. Did kids never speak at a normal volume? "And Gordie had some! It wasn't just me!"

Jared and I both grimaced. Lottie was an incredibly light sleeper and—

"Daddy! Why is the boys eating the cookies?!

Why is the boys being piggies?!" Lottie screamed from her room. "Santa will skip our house! Why are boys so dumb?!"

I blew out a breath that made my lips flap. "So much for that romantic moment. You get the cookies. I'll go put Lottie down. Again."

We'd both crashed after assembling a bike and the magic castle playset from Hell. Even though we were awakened on the sofa at four forty-five in the morning by a jacked-up little girl, the day was a glorious one. Despite a couple of stiff necks and aching backs, we spent Christmas playing with toys, hunting aliens in a new video game system that Soren had requested— for Milo he'd said but Jared and I knew better—and making sure the princess and her magic kitty had a grand adventure. Gordie spent most of the day chewing on a new toy that had been guaranteed to stand up to any puppy. It had not.

We feasted on roast beast—ham, but we liked to be Dr. Seuss-y about it—with all the fixings, and then FaceTime with the families. That night we all collapsed onto our now well-used rec room sofas to watch some animated movie about a princess who rode a kitten and sang in Spanish. The whole movie was in Spanish. Soren, who was in his first year of

Spanish at school assured us he could translate. He could not. But it was a valiant effort.

After the Spanish cat-riding princess flick Jared carried Lottie up to bed while we men settled in for *Ernest Saves Christmas*. Milo conked out before the end credits, so we toted him up the stairs then us three older guys got our sodas and a fresh bag of chips and dove into the ultimate Christmas movie, *Die Hard*.

This time Jared and I were the ones to drift off during the movie. Soren had to wake us up and send us to bed. We stayed awake long enough to give each other those adult presents.

But only just.

"… and then I thought about giving him a macaw," Adler said. "Because I saw this video on Tik Tok where some guy was calling his parrot, which totally looked like a dragon flying through the sky! I mean, how cool was that? Then I recalled Layton might not dig a parrot throwing seeds all over the place, so I changed my mind and bought him a humping animals adult coloring book and a mega box of crayons."

I blinked at Adler as we warmed up, both of us on our knees, stretching out our hamstrings.

"'Humping animals'?" I asked, trying my best not to make a face of any kind.

"Yeah, like elk and bears. You know. Animals." Adler sat on the ice then. I glanced around for someone to come help me, but everyone was skating around, shuttling pucks at Stan, or doing pregame interviews over by the home bench. "It seemed quirky to me. Funny. Do you think he'll like it? Or should I get him something more substantial for Valentine's Day?"

"Um, well…" I reached out over my extended leg to give my brain time to come up with something intelligent. Adler was still seated on the ice, legs splayed out, leaning left then right, his gaze locked on me as he stretched. Damn it. "Well, I got Jared cuff links."

Adler stopped tipping left then right to stare at me from under beetled eyebrows. "Cuff links? That's not really very inventive, is it?"

"I… well, no, I guess not. But then again Jared's not the kind of man who likes quirky inventive things." Actually, he kind of did but I had to assume humping animal coloring books might not be his jam. "He likes cuff links. Wears them all the time." Shit. Now I was doubting my decision on my Valentine's gift for my man. "Do you think I should get him something a little less stuffy?"

"Well, yeah. Oh! Buy him an assortment of flavored lube."

"I'm sorry, what is my ears hearing from here?" Stan asked, skating over to us, his mask up, his face damp with perspiration. "Is talking about fun butt times?"

The woman interviewing Bryan stared at us. Great. My face grew hot.

"No, we are *not* talking about 'fun butt times'," I snapped.

"Well, we kind of were," Adler stated, getting to his skates in one fluid move then offering me a hand up. I thought I might stay on my knees and crawl off the ice if that pretty blonde sportscaster for Tampa Bay kept staring at us with her round blue eyes. "I was telling Ten that cuff links are kind of boring for the big V-Day present. Then I suggested flavored lubes. I bought this ten pack for Layton for his birthday. He loves to be rimmed and—"

"Oh, my gods, guys, really? Can we not have this discussion ten feet from the lady—" I tried to say, then Stan got that happy puppy look that he gets.

"Yes! Erik is loving it much as well. I like the

grape. Is reminding me of jelly. Jam no shakes like that!" Stan roared.

Adler howled in amusement. I started skidding across the ice on my knees, hopefully unseen, but Stan caught me by the jersey then tugged me back into the lube talk.

"Mango is amazing," Adler said while Stan hoisted me to my skates. Ad glanced at me. "You look flushed. Do you have that stomach bug that's going around? Bryan had it last week. Remember he had to leave the game against Buffalo in a hurry because of the explosive—"

"Okay, hey, guys," I hurried to interject as the pretty blonde with the microphone was shuffle-walking across the ice, a glint in her bright blue eyes. "Let's not talk about adult gifts or intestinal afflictions here on the ice. 'Kay? Thanks."

Adler gave me a sour look. "You're not nearly as much fun as you used to be. I think that A on your sweater has stolen all your yuks."

"Has big stick up bumski," Stan chimed in.

"If he used the mango lube that stick would glide in much easier," Adler commented *just* as the nice lady managed to slip-slide her way to us.

"Hi there!" I said as I took her elbow and led her away from the ass conversation taking place by the timekeeper's table. Thank God the poor guy wasn't in his little box. "So, yeah, you want to talk to me?"

"Sure!" She beamed up at me. I took her across the ice to ensure she did not pick up any kind of butt talk. Honestly, it was like trying to herd toddlers out there sometimes.

Sharon, her name was, and I had a nice interview about hockey. No fun butt times were mentioned, and I skated off feeling pretty good about being so fast on my feet. I ran into Jared outside the skate-sharpening room. He nodded at me, his lips tugging upward.

"Hey, so, can I have two minutes?" I asked him. He tipped his head slightly, his brow furrowing. "Nothing's wrong. I mean, I don't think it is. No, it is totally not. I just…" I exhaled strongly, leaned on my stick, and gave the hall a fast look. Everyone had gone back to the locker room to whittle away the time until the game started. "Okay, so I bought you this really nice gift for Valentine's Day."

"Thank you," he replied, leaning closer so we didn't have shout. "I got you something nice too."

"Aw, thanks boo." I smiled at him then got serious again. "See, I got you this nice, practical gift. And I know you're going to like it. But then I got to talking to the guys and they were saying how they got their men all kinds of sexy gifts."

That got his eyebrow to arch. "You know I always kind of assumed you guys were talking about hockey on the ice. I mean we *are* starting to play better after that long painful period before the All-Star break. Now that we're all healed up and back in our assigned lines, I just thought it would be strategy or dissecting plays that you'd be chatting about. Silly me."

I rubbed the back of my damp neck. "I was talking to Adler."

"Ah, okay. That explains it then. Ten, look, I'm not sure what kind of kinky stuff Ad buys for Layton—"

"Flavored lube," I whispered.

His eyes flared. A tiny spark of heat roared to life in those sapphire pools. Which made me a little hard. A totally not cool thing when one was wearing a cup.

"That sounds… interesting," he said as he tugged at his tie.

"Yeah? You think?"

He nodded, his cheeks a little rosier now than they had been. "I think that big online store has next-day delivery." He gave me a saucy wink then strolled off casual as could be.

Shit. I hurried to the locker room, grabbed my phone out of my locker, and placed a fast order to be delivered to our home. It would be there before we were but that was okay. I'd give him the cuff links tomorrow and then the rest of his gift when we were back in Pennsylvania. Smiling as I stared at my phone, it came to me that I was going to have to thank Adler for the idea.

Yeah, I'd not do that until later. Much later. Maybe never.

I couldn't exactly say when it was things fell into place.

Maybe the sportswriters would cite the Railers comeback beginning when Stan made a phenomenal scorpion kick save to deflect a sure goal in the second half of the game.

Maybe the sports bloggers would say the Railers comeback began when Adler Lockhart took out Jamie Rowe with a brutal but legal hip check at the start of the third period.

Maybe the pundits on TV would announce that the Railers comeback had arrived when I'd been on the heels of a Tampa Bay forward moving into their zone when he flagged a bit late in the third. Not much, but enough that I could catch up with him. Coming up on his left, I reached around him, lifting his stick to free the puck. I juked around in a circle, broke away from the man I'd been chasing, puck now on my stick, and sped to the Tampa goal. The goalie had me in his sights as I moved to his left and took a backhanded shot on him. The puck hit the tendie high on his shoulder, dropping to his skates. I braked hard, ice flying, and dove at the puck, using my stick to force it through his legs. He tried to shut it down, slamming his pads to the blue ice but the puck was already in the back of the net when he made his move.

I lay there on the ice, grinning at the red-light flashing, as my teammates appeared around me. They piled on top of me, a mountain of sweaty, stinking men, as if this were the playoffs and not a random game in the middle of a so-so season. I was jerked to my skates then thumped on the back so hard I nearly lost my mouth guard. The fist bumps sailed past, the moment feeling important for some cosmic reason. Deep down, even though it was another possible two points, that goal felt exceptional. It wasn't anything outstanding. Nothing that would make the weekly highlights reel. Yet it had an aura of destiny about it. As if it were to be a catalyst of something great for us.

Taking my seat on the bench, I nodded at the coaches who came over to slap my shoulders. Then, knowing the kids were back home watching on TV—

probably only Soren was up by now, but it was meant for all of them—I looked at the camera lingering on me and tapped my helmet three times. One gentle tap for each of my kids. The brightest stars in my life.

And then, because I knew it would mess with him over the whole stepdad thing, I added another tap for Ryker.

Epilogue

Jared

Soren tugged at his tie and growled in the mirror.

"Stop pulling at it, little bro," Ryker chuckled, and reached around him to straighten it again. I watched my boys—Ryker here for the hearing, said he wouldn't think of being anywhere else. He and Soren texted all the time, and I think it was good that suddenly Soren didn't have all the responsibilities of being the eldest brother.

"I'm not little!" Soren defended, then half smiled at Ryker who gave him a noogie and then had to redo his tie again. They were both in suits—Ryker in one of his most sober post-game ones, Soren in the new suit we'd bought on the weekend. He had a ton of smart clothes, but on Friday he'd asked we get him a suit so the judge would believe what he said. He talked about people hearing what he had to say, and Ten and I never questioned him once.

We never asked what Soren intended to say, and we took him suit-shopping the next day. Of course, Milo tagged along, and looked ridiculously sweet in a suit of his own. Ten was in charge of Lottie, and I hoped she wasn't going to demand to wear an Ariel dress, because courts might frown on Ariel dresses. Right?

Turned out she wanted to go as Soren and Milo's *sister*, which meant flowery leggings and a soft white shirt and purple tie she insisted she was wearing. All four of my children—*our* children—were now in Soren's room, Ten and I hovering at the door, suited and booted with the best of them.

"I think I'm going to cry," Ten whispered as Lottie climbed onto the bed and threw herself into Ryker's arms. He caught her easily, laughing, his curls falling over his eye and Lottie patiently pushing them back.

"Me too," I murmured.

We linked hands, entwining fingers and holding

on tight. Today was the adoption hearing—testimony from Ten and me, testimony from Dale as the case worker, agreement from Soren, as he was over the age of twelve, and then the court would issue an adoption decree and certificate of adoption. Then the boys would officially be ours, and we'd have new birth certificates issued in their new adoptive names. Soren and Milo Madsen-Rowe. *Our* sons. Soren had been practicing a speech for the judge, but given what Dale told us, all he had to really say was that he agreed he wanted to stay with us.

In six months, the angry, confused young man had learned he was safe and loved with us, and I didn't imagine for one minute he would say he didn't want to stay, but it was still nerve-wracking. This was the moment we'd worked toward; the last six months had been scary, and exciting, and I had so much love to give all four of our children that sometimes I thought I would burst.

"Madsen-Rowes is to be coming quick snap!" Stan called up to us. There was some shushing from someone sounding like Erik, a curse word from Adler, more mumbling, and then the six of us headed downstairs. All of our friends were here, the hearing luckily enough fell on a day with no game, and a short practice Ten and me had been given dispensation to miss. Everyone else had turned up immediately after said practice anyway.

We were heading for the Stanley Cup finals—our first head-to-head was in three days against Columbus, a match up I wasn't looking forward to, given how strong Columbus was. At least we weren't meeting Boston first, but if they defeated New York, and we passed Columbus, then they'd be next. Tension was high, the team was amped up, Connor was back, Stan in net, Bryan backing him up, Ten was on fire… hell, we might go all the way.

But first, and more importantly for us both, was today.

The convoy of cars struggled parking, but we had priority and the six of us were first in court, the rest of the team coming in as they could, until the whole contingent of Madsen-Rowes' and extended friends and family were seated and waiting.

Judge Geraldton was a kindly woman, gentle almost. She perused the files, checked the relevant paperwork, and then called Ten for his statement. He spoke of his pride in Soren and Milo, and he confirmed that he wanted to adopt. Then it was me, and I was nervous as I would be in game seven of the cup final.

"Jared Madsen-Rowe," I identified myself, then

said my bit about what I wanted to do. I didn't have to say anything else, but I tagged it on anyway. "We love Soren and Milo and can't wait to be their fathers."

Then it was Soren, who after whispering with Ryker for a moment, rose. The judge asked him his opinion of where he'd like to be, and he reached a hand for Milo who stood up also, then for Ryker, who not only got to his feet but gathered Lottie into his arms.

Together the four of them stood quietly, and when they were all up, Soren tipped his chin.

"Soren. My name is Soren Madsen-Rowe. I want to stay with Jared and Tennant Madsen-Rowe." He cleared his throat, then stared at us instead of the judge, and we all waited expectantly as Ryker squeezed his shoulder and Milo grinned at him, and Lottie clapped her hands.

"This is the easiest thing I've ever had to say," he continued. "If they'll have me, have *us*, then I want to stay with my new dads."

And there wasn't a dry eye in the house.

———

Read **Soren** and **Felix's** story in a brand-new Scott/Locey Young Adult novel, coming 2023

Read **Westy** and **Levi's** FREE story in the December Advent event featuring over fifty authors –

Sign up for news on release of both here - mmhockeyromance.com/subscribe

Free Story

Read Westy and Levi's story in Christmas Promises - FREE

Christmas Promises

When the world falls from beneath his feet, Levi escapes pitying glances and awkward questions by renting a cabin in Big Bear. When his old flame James turns up on his doorstep, the promise they made to stay apart is shattered, and somehow love takes hold.

Five years ago, sniping and competing turned to passion when Levi and James kissed. They had their whole lives ahead of them, but hockey was everything and when they were drafted to different sides of the country, they knew their relationship could go no further, and promised it would end and never be mentioned again.

But when cancer strikes, Levi faces uncertain times as his career crumbles and his life is turned upside down. There is only one thing he's certain of, and that is he doesn't need James or the promise he made to come back in his life. Right?

Family First (Railers 13)

An injury threatens to end Stan's career. Will he choose to fight for his beloved hockey, or put his family first?

Few goalies are as dedicated as Stan Lyamin, known for his resilience on the ice, talking to his pipes, and his love of Elvis. Add in his adoration of his family and his life has been filled with all the things that bring him joy. However, after a heart-wrenching game ends with a disastrous hip injury, Stan faces the most challenging obstacle of his career: surgery, an extensive recovery, and the looming threat of retirement. It's now that he has to decide which path to take: the one that will lead him back to the game he adores or the one that will see his jersey lifted to the rafters.

Erik and Stan, once invincible with the Railers, have always skated through life's challenges hand in hand. Their love story, cemented by a shared passion for hockey and the joy of raising their children, has been their shield against the world. But when their son Noah's life is changed forever by a medical diagnosis, this forever love is put to the test. Erik turns to his husband for support, but Stan is consumed with guilt, overwhelmed by decisions, and retreats into himself when his family needs him the most.

Free Reads

Please note - in all of these free stories, there will be some spoilers for the main series books.

Railers Short Stories

Volume 1 | Volume 2

LA Storm

Sparkle

The Colts - AHL Short Stories

Pucks & Percentages

Breakaway

Making the Save

Standalone

Waiting for Christmas

When hockey wunderkind Tennant Rowe meets his new coach, he knows he's in trouble. Jared Madsen is nine years older than Tennant, impossibly attractive, and — worst of all — his brother's off-limits best friend. Is their chemistry worth the risk?

Changing Lines (Railers 1)

Can Tennant show Jared that age is just a number, and that love is all that matters?

The Rowe Brothers are famous hockey hotshots, but as the youngest of the trio, Tennant has always had to play against his brothers' reputations. To get out of their shadows, and against their advice, he accepts a trade to the Harrisburg Railers, where he runs into Jared Madsen. Mads is an old family friend and his brother's one-time teammate. Mads is Tennant's new coach. And Mads is the sexiest thing he's ever laid eyes on.

Jared Madsen's hockey career was cut short by a fault in his heart, but coaching keeps him close to the game. When Ten is traded to the team, his carefully organized world is thrown into chaos. Nine years his junior and his best friend's brother, he knows Ten is strictly off-limits, but as soon as he sees Ten's moves, on and off the ice, he knows that his heart could get him into trouble again.

Changing Lines

Harrisburg Railers (Hockey Romance)

7. Neutral Zone
8. Hat Trick
9. Save The Date
10. Baby Makes Three
11. Rivals
12. Perfect Gifts
13. Family First

Railers Volume 1 | Railers Volume 2 | Railers Volume 3 | Railers Volume 4

Meet the men of Owatonna University's hockey team

Ryker (Owatonna U, 1)

Ryker

Ryker is hockey royalty, Jacob is a poor country boy. Can two vastly different people find common ground and become the men they want to be?

Ryker comes from a long line of championship-winning

hockey players. Playing college hockey to develop his game is his only focus, and nothing will stand in the way of him working to become the best player. He has no room for relationships, people who point out his flaws, or anyone who calls him on his dreams. He certainly has no place for love, and meeting Jacob is nothing but a useful distraction on the side. After all trying to get his Owatonna Eagles teammate into bed is less work and more play. When tragedy rocks his family, his charmed life crumbles, and the only person he can turn to is the same one who claims to hate him.

Jacob Benson has only known hard work and stifling conservative values his whole life. Born and raised in the small rural community of Eden Crossing, Minnesota, he's the only son of a hard-working but struggling dairy farming family. Jacob is using his skills in hockey to finance his way to an agricultural science degree. These four years at Owatonna U. will probably be the only time he has to enjoy life, gain acceptance about his sexuality, and live openly before his inevitable return to the farm. Running into a pretty rich boy like Ryker Madsen is putting a damper on his enjoyment of life away from home. Ryker's flip, conceited, carefree attitude grates on Jacob's every nerve. So why, if Ryker is everything he dislikes, does he want nothing more than to explore the sinful dreams that his annoying teammate stars in every night?

Ryker

Owatonna U Hockey (Hockey Romance)

1. Ryker
2. Scott
3. Benoit
4. Christmas Lights
5. Valentine's Hearts
6. Desert Dreams

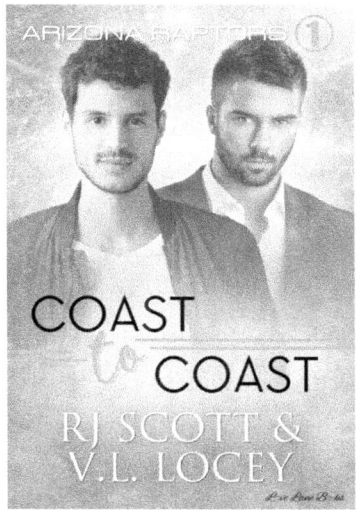

Coast to Coast (Arizona Raptors 1)

Coast To Coast

When opposites attract, this bottom-of-the-league team will never be the same again.

A stipulation in his father's will forces Mark back into the arms of a family that disowned him and leaves him one-third owner of a hockey team facing financial ruin. He doesn't even watch hockey, let alone like it, and wants nothing more than to head back to New York. Then there's the new coach, a stubborn, opinionated, irritating man with superiority issues and questionable music taste. Butting heads with Rowen becomes the new normal, but it comes with passionate debate and an all-consuming lust.

Challenged to rebuild one of the worst teams in the league into a future cup contender, Rowen can't pass up the opportunity. Never in his twenty years of hockey has he ever seen a team managed so badly or coached players overflowing with resentment and bigotry. Yet there's something about this team and this city that compels him to roll up his sleeves and start dismantling. If only Mark, one of three siblings who now own the Raptors, wasn't so damned rock-headed yet so damned appealing his job might be easier. It doesn't look like either is willing to give in, but one night in a dark, desert hotel changes everything.

Coast To Coast

Arizona Raptors (Hockey Romance)

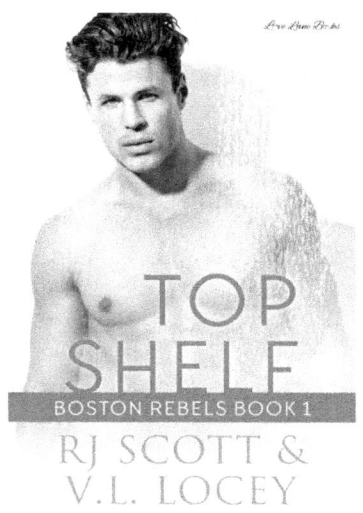

Top Shelf (Boston Rebels 1)

Acting on the attraction to his best friend's brother has always been off the table for Xander until a passionate hookup with Mason at a beach resort begins a love affair that burns long after summer ends.

Mason specializes in assisting same-sex couples on their journey to becoming parents and fighting every rule that blocks his way in the stuck-in-the-past agency that hired him. Living in his brother's pool house is rent-free, and every cent he earns he saves for his dream—that one day he'd have his own company helping others. The downside is that he has to see his annoying brother every day, the upside is that his brother's teammates from the Boston Rebels make regular visits. The eye candy that passes Mason's window is almost enough to make him consider dating a hockey player, but not just any player though. Ever since Xander—his brother's childhood friend—came out as gay at a press conference, Mason's puppy love has turned into a burning attraction he can no longer ignore.

Hockey has been one of Xander's main focuses since he was old enough to balance on skates. Well, hockey and Mason Kingsley, but Mason was always unattainable. Now that he's about to see thirty candles on his birthday cake and is no longer hiding the fact he's gay, he's ready to find a soul mate to make his life complete. A summer vacation is just what he needs to have time to think, but when the Boston Rebels arriving in paradise with Mason in tow, thinking is the last thing he needs. One torrid night under a balmy moon and rules about not messing with his best friend's brother vanish on a warm, tropical breeze.

Summer romances don't generally last past Labor Day, but with the new season about to begin Xander and Mason are going to have to face the world and decide if their love is real enough to withstand everything.

Boston Rebels

Lost In Boston (Free Prequel Novella)

1. Top Shelf
2. Back Check
3. Snowed
4. Royal Lines
5. Blade
6. Rental

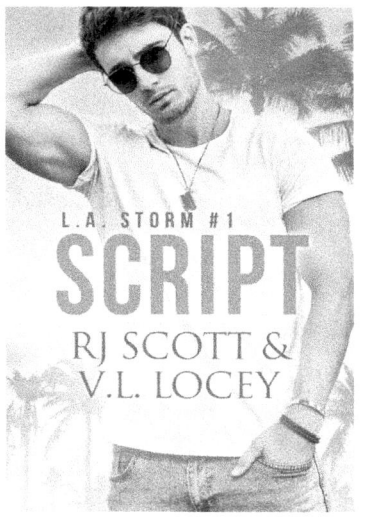

Script (LA Storm, 1)

Script

Hollywood A-lister Finn might be Canadian, but he needs Cameron to show him how to hockey.

Actor Finn Kerrigan is at a crossroads. After growing up a soap star, then starring in a hugely successful trilogy of action movies, he's finally given the chance to read a heartfelt and passionate script that could change his life forever. The role would be enough for people to see him as a serious actor, and maybe even win him an award or two (and no, a golden raspberry award for his action movies doesn't count). Once established as a serious actor he's sure he can come out of the closet and finally live his truth.

When he lies to get the part of a hockey player on a struggling team, he suddenly has nowhere to hide. He might be Canadian, but the last time he skated he was ten, and no, he doesn't have hockey in his blood. With only a month until filming starts, he about to be exposed, but partnered with a player who's supposed to be giving him tips, he doesn't realize how many of his secrets will come to light. Falling in lust, one heated kiss at a time, is inevitable, but giving Cameron up at the end of the shoot could break his heart.

Cameron Chavkin is the face of the LA Storm. And the body, and the hair, and the smile. He's at the prime of his career, men and women want to be with him, and he's skating better than he ever has before. His house sits next to a famous rock star's mansion, his garage is filled with expensive cars, and he's even been asked to mentor a once-famous actor in a new hockey movie. Life is pretty sweet. Until the bad boy of hockey meets Finn, a man on the edge with more secrets than Cameron has endorsements. Knowing better than to get involved, Cameron is swept up despite himself, and when it's time to say goodbye to the Storm's most eligible bachelor is finding it hard to follow the script.

Script

LA Storm

1. Script
2. Second
3. Shield
4. Spiral

Off The Ice (Chesterford Coyotes, 1)

Off The Ice

**A coming-of-age love story with high school, hockey
rivalry, friendship, family, and coming out.**

Soren's life changes in an instant when he and his younger
brother are adopted by hockey royalty. Making sense of his
new life is hard enough, but when he's enrolled in a private
school it means facing a whole new set of problems.

Navigating friendship, family, and hockey is one thing, but being attracted to the boy who vexes him is a whole new thing.

Felix has a reputation to protect. He's the kid who seems to have everything but looks can be deceiving. Spinning lies about his perfect life, he's created a fantasy world that even he has started to believe. Only, it's not long before everything crumbles, all of his pretty lies are revealed, and only his closest rival sees through his pain and stands by him.

Fighting is easy, friendship is hard, but love is everything.

Off The Ice

Chesterford Coyotes

Also By RJ Scott

For a full list of ebooks and links please scan the code
above or visit rjscott.co.uk/rjbooks

Meet RJ Scott

RJ discovered romance in books at a very young age and realized that if there wasn't romance on the page, she could create it in her head. With over one hundred and fifty books published, she is a full time author of gay romance.

She lives and works out of her home in the beautiful English countryside, spends her spare time reading, watching films, and enjoying time with her family.

The last time she had a week's break from writing she didn't like it one little bit and has yet to meet a box of chocolates she couldn't defeat.

www.rjscott.co.uk | rj@rjscott.co.uk

NEWSLETTER - rjscott.co.uk/rjnews

facebook.com/author.rjscott

x.com/Rjscott_author

instagram.com/rjscott_author

amazon.com/author/rj-scott

bookbub.com/authors/rj-scott

goodreads.com/rjscott

pinterest.com/rjscottauthor

Also By VL Locey

For a full list of ebooks and links please scan the code
above or visit vllocey.com/stories-from-vl-locey

Meet V.L. Locey

V.L. Locey loves worn jeans, yoga, belly laughs, walking, reading and writing lusty tales, Greek mythology, the New York Rangers, comic books, and coffee.

(Not necessarily in that order.)

She shares her life with her husband, her daughter, one dog, two cats, a flock of assorted domestic fowl, and two Jersey steers.

When not writing spicy romances, she enjoys spending her day with her menagerie in the rolling hills of Pennsylvania with a cup of fresh java in hand.

vllocey.com
vicki@vllocey.com

Newsletter - vllocey.com/newsletter

facebook.com/V.L.Locey

x.com/vllocey

instagram.com/vl_locey

bookbub.com/authors/v-l-locey

goodreads.com/vllocey

pinterest.com/vllocey